THE DEADLY
DETECTIVE AGENCY

Abigail Summers Cozy Mysteries
Book 1

ANN PARKER

With love and gratitude to Terry, Emma, Louise, and all my grandchildren.

With a special thanks to Helen Bennett and all my friends on the XYL net.

Lastly, a big thank you to Next Chapter Publishing and their fantastic team.

Becklesfield is a picturesque market town nestled at the base of the Chiltern Hills in the south of England. The church dates back to the 16th century. Market days are Tuesday and Saturday. The High Street boasts a good selection of small shops, a Grade 2 listed library, and two pubs. The latest census recorded the parish's population as 3,256. At some point during the last two days, that figure dropped to 3,255.

Chapter 1

ABIGAIL SUMMERS FELT STRANGELY REFRESHED WHEN she woke up. She felt like she had been asleep for days, but still told herself, 'two more minutes' and snuggled back down again. Ah, there was nothing like lying in or having a duvet day on... Sunday? Monday? She wasn't sure, and what time was it? Abigail looked over at the clock - just before eight. But was that morning or evening? Morning surely. Did she overdo the white wine again last night? She could remember a headache, thinking about it. She shot out of bed as someone slowly opened the door. She was about to pick up the lamp to hit them over the head when she recognised the person. "Monica? What on earth are you doing here?"

"Look at the mess in here. I say we dump everything. Especially all the bedding."

"And the bed. I couldn't sleep in that now," said a voice she knew well.

Abigail's heart almost stopped, and she started to wonder if it had. She had always prided herself on her powers of perception, but in her defence, she hadn't been ill and hadn't even seen a doctor for the past twelve years. Maybe she should have, thinking about it.

Her nephew, Aaron, and his ghastly wife, Monica, were rummaging through her things, of all the cheek.

"Bin. Bin. Charity. No, bin. Bin."

"What the hell are you doing?" shrieked Abigail. "Monica, I mean it, if you don't stop..." But Monica didn't stop. Monica, she realised, could not see her. Abigail walked over to the mirror, but she couldn't make herself out clearly either, until a mist cleared. I'm dreaming, totally doolally or dead. She sat on the bed to think which one. Surely if she had died, her body would be lying there, like the ghost in the film. Anyway, she can't possibly be dead. She was only in her late thirties and had loads to do for work, and she hadn't been married yet, not even engaged. Aaron, who although he was the sole beneficiary in her will, hadn't been in touch for well over a year. Now here was his money-grabbing wife rummaging through her things. So not dreaming or doolally then, she thought. But maybe dead. She hadn't been ill, had she? No, she was never ill. Although she did kind of remember a bad headache and dizziness at some point. She'd find out what had happened if it was the last thing she did. Oh God, what was the last thing she did?

Aaron had a look on the dressing table. "Any jewellery that's worth anything?"

"No, not much. Most of it is cheap tat, just costume jewellery. No engagement ring, of course," she said and laughed.

"Do you mind, that's my cheap tat." Abigail lunged towards her, but her hand went straight through her. "Either you're dead or me." When it did the same to her keepsake box when she went to snatch it off Aaron, she began to think that it must be her. Aww, that's a shame she thought. "I'm too young. What about all my TV shows I'm halfway through? I can't believe this is happening. I wonder if it was that pizza I heated up. It had been hanging about for a few days. So what does one actually do when one is dead?" She had another look in the mirror. She looked alright, a bit flushed. Not stabbed or anything awful like that. Oh, and her hair looked okay. She turned to the side. A bit of bed-hair at the back but nothing too bad, and the fact that her shoulder-length blonde hair was curly hid it pretty well. "At least I coloured it last week. Damn, I had those brand new cream, silk pyjamas that I was saving for best. Why couldn't I have been wearing those? Oh my God, shut up, Abigail. I'm so vain, even when I'm dead!"

She wasn't scared, sorry, or frightened. Sort of excited, peaceful, and with a kind of warmth. First of all, she tried walking through a wall - no trouble there. She managed the stairs without incident. So far so good. What have they done to the kitchen? A big pile of food was on the table and some in the bin. She'd only bought that carrot cake last week. The sitting room was similarly upturned. Don't say she was stuck here for an eternity with these two. She'd take Hell. But could she leave the house? Abigail closed her eyes and went through the front door. She felt sad and happy at the same time.

She stopped and looked back at her childhood home. It was an old listed building that was now painted white, but the lattice windows in the original wooden frames remained as they were over one hundred years ago. She only hoped Aaron didn't have plans to rip them out and put plastic ones in. Even the front door was the same one as when it was built, although the huge keyhole was now redundant in favour of a Yale lock. She remembered the day when she was about six, that her father had nailed a horseshoe at the top of it. "It's got to point upwards, Abi, so the luck stays in." Until this day, she always felt it had. With a big sigh, she walked away.

Abigail suddenly remembered that she was in her red pyjamas. But after a pushchair had been pushed through her and a car had driven past, she realised she was indeed a ghost of the very dead kind and no one could see her anymore. Was she the only one? What should she do now? Abigail had lived in Beck-lesfield all her life and was thinking she should have travelled more when she had the chance. The thought of those two being in there was too much to bear. She would be turning in her grave - if she had one. Oh, perhaps she did have one. Maybe that's the first place she should go.

She walked to the old church that she had been christened in and where her family were buried. It was next to the village green which was busy with parents walking their children to the small primary school that she had attended. No one seemed to see her, although she could swear that a couple of the smaller children looked at her and smiled. She walked around the pond to the stone wall that surrounded the church. It was too early for Reverend Stevens to be there, but there was a middle-aged man looking down by one of the graves. Abigail went over to where her mother, father, and brother had been buried. No open grave or sign of hers. That was a relief at least. Perhaps she was dreaming or having an out-of-body, or rather an out-of-house experience. Should she be looking for a light or a tunnel? Or maybe her mum and dad? She'd go into the church first before she really started to panic. The church clock chimed nine as she followed the path to the wooden, arched door and stood in the porch. "Good job I didn't sleep in the nuddy," Abigail said out loud.

"You wouldn't be the first," said the man who had been in the graveyard, and funnily enough, also wearing pyjamas of the striped variety. The handsome, in a rugged way gentleman had noticed the rather attractive woman wandering up and down outside the church and felt he had to help her.

"You can see me?" asked a very relieved Abigail. "Oh my, I can see you too. Are you a ghost as well, or are we both nuts?"

"Well, I may be a bit of both," he laughed. "The name's Terry. Are you a newly departed? Or should I say a recently arrived?"

"I'm not actually sure. The first thing I knew about it, my nephew's wife was clearing out my things. And being very rude about my stuff. I'm Abigail Summers."

"It can take a while for the spirit to leave the body. And don't worry if you can't remember how you died. That's perfectly normal. It's a bit like a head injury when patients never can remember what happened when they come round. For a while anyway."

"I was rather expecting to go to Heaven, if I'm honest."

"In my experience, over the last fifty odd years of being dead, is that sudden death from an illness or an accident is the second biggest cause of being stuck here."

"What's the first?"

"Murder," he said.

"I love a whodunnit as much as anyone else, but I really don't think I was murdered. I'm sorry to say that I'm not that important. Although my nephew, Aaron does seem to have inherited my house rather quickly!"

Terry sighed, "I've seen people roaming these streets for a ten-pound note, so I'd keep an open mind if I was you."

"I will, for sure. I don't want him getting away with murder. It was my family home. I've got all my memories inside those walls and in that garden. It will break my heart and my parents' if he moves in there. But he's the only family I've got now. His dad, my brother, died a few years back. Apart from the night attire, how did you know I was dead?" asked Abigail.

"Look at me. Can you see a slight aura around me?"

"Yes, I can. I had noticed that already. Are there many of us about?"

"Not as many as you'd think. Most people go straight to where they're supposed to be. Or some people like me have the chance to leave and don't take it. If you like, I can introduce you to my friends. I'll show you where we all hang out. It may surprise you."

They walked past the village shop and into the high street. Life had gone on without her, Abigail thought sadly. Was this how it was going to be from now on; she was simply a spectator? Watching the world but not being able to be part of it. Mrs Merry was putting her flowers outside her shop, while the Post Office opened its door and Mr. Banning from the antique shop was chatting and laughing with Cassie Briggs. Surely Cassie should be grieving - obviously not. Terry gestured to her to enter a building which Abigail had not been in for years. "The Becklesfield Public Library? That's hardly gothic or ghostly," she said.

"Where else are there newspapers, computers, a television to look at and an ever-changing group of visitors? We can keep up with all the current events. Not forgetting we get the place to ourselves after hours. All my friends come here. Come on, I'll introduce you," said Terry.

The building was one of the oldest in the village and was spread over two floors. The library itself was open plan and the reference and the storage rooms were upstairs. It had not opened its doors to the public yet but towards the back of the large room, a group of people were sitting in some comfy chairs.

"Everyone, this is our latest arrival, Abigail."

She met Betty, who was a sprightly lady of eighty-two, dressed in beige trousers and a striped jumper. "Welcome, my dear. I expect you're a touch confused but you're amongst friends. Come and sit next to me."

Jim, a recently deceased builder, was a muscly young man in a denim jacket and khaki jeans with pockets down both of the legs. She then met Suzie, a pretty, young black girl in a flowery dress. And lastly, Nurse Lillian, who was wearing her navy uniform. Her watch was still pinned to her chest and Abigail noticed her black shoes were rather muddy and she thought a Matron would not have liked that. They were all excited to meet someone else. It could get a bit boring sometimes.

"I would say I'm pleased to meet you, but I can't help feeling I would have preferred not to. So let me get this straight. I was never very good at names. Terry, I remember. Then it's Betty, Suzie, Lillian and Jim?"

Terry congratulated her. "That's right, well done. Now listen, Abigail wants to find out how she died. I said we could help her." They all agreed.

"I'm dying to know...sorry, an unintended pun, if my nephew and his wife, Aaron and Monica have done something. Was it a sudden illness or was I even murdered? I've always been healthy and hardly ever even got a cold."

"You know what they say, a creaking gate hangs longest," said Betty, who had a wealth of sayings, but not always said them in the right way.

"What does that mean?" asked Abigail.

"I've no idea, but that's what they say."

Terry thought he knew. "I think it means that those who have a lot of illnesses usually outlive those that are healthy. Although it sounds a bit backwards to me."

"All I know is that I'm sure this gate should still be hanging. My hinges were fine, thank you very much. I need to know what went wrong. It must affect your quality of life, or death now you're here."

"Well, if it makes you feel better," said Betty, "I didn't read about your murder in the Chiltern Weekly, so chances are it was a natural death. And it wasn't in the obituaries, although that probably won't make you feel better."

"I'd have thought someone would have put it in there and said, 'Sadly missed' or 'Family flowers only' or something. Aaron, my nephew, wouldn't if you had to pay. And to be fair, my parents and brother have passed. And I finished with my boyfriend last month. Typical. No one cares."

"Well, you have us now," said Terry. "Tell us something about yourself, Abigail."

"I'm… well, I was thirty-nine. At least I'll never be forty, thinking on the bright side. I do sewing alterations and dress-making, working from home. That's about it. See what I mean, Terry? Who would want to murder me?"

Jim said excitedly, "Perhaps you saw or heard something. Or they were after your money. Did you disturb a burglar? Or it could have been a madman."

"Let me have a look at you," said Nurse Lillian. "I can't see any signs of violence or external injuries. No bruises, blood, or broken bones, although you look rather red. I died of a heart attack, so you might be the same. Or it could be poison, I suppose."

"Or strangulation," said Jim.

"There would still be signs of that. Marks around your throat. Maybe they put a pillow over your face," suggested Terry helpfully.

"Oh dear, I'm hoping it was just a heart attack now," Abigail told them.

"Tell me about it," said Jim. He turned round, and Abigail gasped when she saw a bloody gash in his back.

"Oh my God, I'm so sorry, Jim. Is that from a knife? Who did it?"

"I haven't got a clue. I can't remember, and there's nothing in the papers."

"And if it's not in the papers, it is because they haven't found his body yet," added Terry. "At least someone knows you're dead, Abigail. Someone must have cared enough to go into your house and find you."

"I can't think who. Unless it was Aaron after he murdered me. It could be the postman if I couldn't sign for something. I have got a slight problem ordering things online. More than likely it was a customer, and the only reason she did anything was that she wanted to collect her sewing that I'd done. I wonder if the police broke down the door. Or smashed a window."

She had always liked to know what was going on. Nosy, actually, she thought. Was that what had got her killed? She loved a good gossip with her customers. But it was more that she liked to hear what they'd been up to, she told herself. Not nosy, caring, that was it.

"I was in the paper when I was run over," said Suzie proudly. "And when the driver got sent to prison for drunk driving."

"I'm so sorry to hear that. I feel a bit guilty now. How old are you?"

"I'm nine. And I was so looking forward to being ten. I was on the way to my friend's birthday party. It was a crossing, and maybe I should have been looking, but he was going so fast. It was my poor mummy I felt sorry for. I got to the hospital but died soon after that."

"That's when I found her," said Lillian. We've stayed together ever since."

"She's lucky to have you, Lillian. You all seem so lovely. But I really need to find out what happened to me, or else I'll never rest in peace. I kind of remember a headache and even a bit of a cough but nothing else. I'm going back to my house to check out some things. Who's coming?" Terry and Suzie jumped up and said, "We're in. See you later."

"Now what was that saying my old mum used to say?" said Betty. "About a cough. It was something like - It's not the coughing that carries your coffin; it's the... No, that's not it. It's not the cough that carries you off; it's the coffin... I think I'm getting closer. It's not the cough that... It's..."

"...going to be a long day," sighed Lillian.

Chapter 2

LESS THAN TWO MILES AWAY, JESSICA GREEN CAME TO
and opened her eyes. It was so dark that she wondered if she
had gone blind, then the room started to spin. After a few
seconds, she could make out something above her head... some
kind of window. Definitely not home then. She had never been
anywhere so dark. Even at night, the glow from the streetlights
usually lit up the sky. Where the hell was she? Her mind was
blank. Why did she feel so ill? Her head hurt like crazy and was
fuzzy. "I'm going to throw up," she thought. "Must be the
booze." She knew the feeling from when she went to Isla's party
when she was seventeen, and her parents had gone away. She
swore then that she would never mix wine and vodka.

All Jessica could do was feel around. On a bed - single. The
edge was hard and cold, as was the headboard, and she realised
it was made from steel. The mattress was thin, like the type you
get in prison. "Oh my God, is that it? I've been arrested?"

Her eyes got used to the dark, and she could make out the
shape of the room, but little else. The ceiling sloped, so not a
cell then. She wasn't sure whether to be pleased or not. It
smelled disgusting as well. She knew that smell from when she

used to visit her great-grandma, damp and old clothes. A wave of nausea and dizziness came over her again. She put her head back on the pillow. Jessica was freezing cold, but beads of sweat formed on her forehead. She felt around for a blanket, but there wasn't one. Who would leave her without a blanket? Someone bad was the only answer. For the first time in her life, she knew what it meant to say a chill went down your spine.

Jessica felt the little bit of strength she had drain from her body. Her muscles felt like lead, her arm too heavy to move the strand of long dark hair that covered her face.

She kept as quiet as a mouse so she could hear if she was alone. Or was her captor hidden in one of the corners of the room? "Hello. Is someone here?" she whispered.

Her question was answered by a gust of wind that rattled the glass in the old window frame above her, and the whole house creaked. The deadly silence soon returned, and her head started throbbing to the loud beat of her heart. Why couldn't she think what had happened to her? She had a vague recollection of a date at a pub and a man with a beard but nothing else. She might have been twenty-two, but she'd never wanted her mum so much in all her life. Jessica tried to shout out in case someone was there that could save her, but only a croak escaped her parched throat and dry lips. Tears ran down her face, and she licked at those for a bit of moisture. Salt was the last thing that she tasted before she once again entered into the realms of unconsciousness.

Chapter 3

ABIGAIL FELT LIKE SHE SHOULD KNOCK OR something, but in the end, she just closed her eyes and stormed through the door. It was still her house, after all. Aaron, a short, slightly balding man in his late twenties, was sitting on her sofa like the King of the castle.

"I can't believe they've just taken over like this. Talk about jumping on my grave, and I'm not even in it yet."

Aaron looked haughtily around the room that had once been Abigail's favourite place. "We'll have to decorate as well. No offence, but her taste is horrendous. And it's so draughty. Let's rip out those old wooden windows and put plastic ones in. I'm freezing all of a sudden."

"We can't change anything until we inherit properly. It's still in her name until the inquest is over," said the thin-lipped Monica. "Thank goodness we found the will. That means it can all go through nice and quick. I can't wait to find out how much money she's got. Her statements show she's got a few thousand in her main account, but I reckon she's got some hidden away somewhere."

"I'm glad you found that cash box in her sideboard. That will help a bit with the move," added Aaron.

"That was my sewing money. I worked hard for that," Abigail muttered.

"I can't believe she didn't have a carbon monoxide alarm. Everybody knows it's called the invisible killer," said Monica.

"I won't be bloody invisible if I find out it was you," shouted Abigail, even though they couldn't hear her.

"Who doesn't have one of them these days? Still good news for us," as they both laughed.

Abigail exploded at that. "Of course I had one, you silly woman. Actually, I've got two. One at the top of the stairs and one by the boiler. I'll show you." She had forgotten they couldn't hear her, but Terry said to show him.

"Here in the kitchen near the boiler. Oh my God, it's gone. You can see where it was. There's a brand new one over there, though, that's not mine. Let me check upstairs… Gone as well. They were laughing about it, weren't they? They actually killed me, Terry. I died a slow death of carbon monoxide poisoning! That's why I had a headache and was out of it."

"They didn't admit to it. They laughed, but they didn't say they had done it. And they would have had to tinker with the boiler. Would they have known how to do that?"

"He's an engineer, so definitely, Terry. But you're right, that's not proof. I wish I could actually haunt them. Throw that bottle at them or something. I can't, can I?" she said with an evil look in her eye.

"I can," said Suzie. "I'm a Mover. That's what we call it. I can move things around and pick things up. Might be because I'm a kid."

"Amazing. Right, what shall we do? See the vase next to him, can you push it into his lap?"

Without answering, little Suzie did just that, and a

screaming Aaron jumped in the air. For some reason, Monica got the blame. Serves her right, thought Abigail.

"I just want to have a last look around before we go. I don't want to come back while they're here. This is my sewing room, Suzie. These are the jobs that I've done," she said, pointing to a rail of clothes. "And these are ones I've got to do. At least I won't have to now. There's going to be some unhappy people in the next few weeks when they don't get their alterations back. This is my bedroom."

"It's pretty. I like the wallpaper," said Suzie.

"It was before it was taken over by black bags. This one's full of my shoes! I can't believe she'd get rid of my best red ones."

"Maybe her enormous big hooves won't get in them."

"Very true. Thank you for that, Suzie. One more thing before we go... I must read the end of that Inspector Parker book. Please, could you turn a few pages for me? At least I will know who dun that one. And tomorrow, I'll start investigating my own murder."

Before the day started on the following morning, Abigail got her newly found friends to meet in the library's staff room. Terry, Jim, Betty, Nurse Lillian, and Suzie sat around in a circle.

"I feel like I'm in the middle of a whodunnit book, and the last chapter is missing. So I'm hoping, between us, we can solve it. Kind of like 'Murder, She Wrote' style."

"Murder who wrote?" asked Terry.

"After your time, I'm afraid. It was a TV show with a different murder every week, and an author solved it. Perhaps one night Suzie could get the television going, and we'll all watch it. I'm basically saying we can investigate ourselves. Find some clues, etc."

"I loved that program," said Betty. "Never missed an episode. I've always wanted to be a sloth."

"I think you mean sleuth, my dear," said Terry.

Betty had a habit of mixing up her words as well as her sayings and sighed, "That's what I said. I do know that we need suspects and a motive. Did you see something you shouldn't have? Is it revenge or jealousy? Or for money."

"Or for love," said Suzie.

"I'm in between boyfriends at the moment. Although the next one is looking ever more unlikely. And the last one dumped me, so I don't think he would care enough to do anything. That's a bit sad, now that I think of it."

"Could have been a serial killer," said Lillian.

Jim shook his head. "They don't usually kill by carbon monoxide poisoning. They like to be there at the kill, as it were."

"Good point," agreed Terry. "So the week before you died, what did you do, Abigail? Did you meet any dodgy people or see anyone being attacked?"

"Not that I know of. I didn't have a date, I'm embarrassed to say. The only time I saw anyone was to do with sewing. Or the supermarket. I've got a better social life now, actually."

Betty sat up straighter, "Come on then, give us some suspects."

"I did the weekly delivery to Brooks Boutique to drop off their alterations and picked up an evening dress and two pairs of trousers. I wonder what happened to them. Oh well, I don't care. I can't see the two ladies that run it being suspects. Gwen from next door came round. She's lived there for twenty years, and we've never had a problem. I've been altering the outfit for her son's wedding. She tried it on with the hat and shoes, then I made us a coffee, and about an hour later she went off, more than happy with what I had done."

"If she was your neighbour, did she have a spare key?" asked Lillian.

"Yes, she did. But I can't think of any reason for wanting me out of the way. Unless she wanted her son to move into my house. But there are far easier ways. Where was I? Of course, I did a home visit to a very good client of mine - Lady Helen Hatton at Chiltern Hall."

"Ooh, very posh," said Suzie.

"She is. And actually very nice. Not a snob at all, like some. I was there to alter her dress for the May Day Fayre they're having in the grounds. It just needed turning up and the waist taken in an inch or two. We went into her bedroom, or the master bedroom, as she called it, because I had to give her a quote for the curtains she had bought, which were too long. With all their money, she always wanted a price first. Frightened to death she was going to pay over the odds. Must be worrying for her with all the millions they've got. And I'll tell you, all the work that I've done for her over the years, she hasn't ever given me a tip."

Jim, the builder, knew just what she meant. "I know. I did some remodelling there once, and I didn't get a penny extra. Yet the number of pensioners that say 'Here you are, Jim, have a drink on me'. Not only that, I prefer cash, and they always insisted on cheques or bank transfers. They can claim it against their taxes then. No thought that I might not want to put it on mine. They just don't have a clue what it's like to struggle."

"Exactly. The more money they have, the more they keep. Well, I pinned her dress, and then she said her husband, Lord Angus, had got some golf trousers that needed shortening and her son, Charles, had got a shirt he wanted taking in. She said the young were so vain, and he hadn't taken any notice when she said there was nothing wrong with it - as usual. So she went off to get them. Of course, I had a bit of a nose while I was waiting. It's a lovely room."

"Tell us what you saw. There could be a clue or a red earring," said Betty.

"A red what? A red earring?" asked Suzie.

"She means a red herring," said Lillian, laughing. "It's a clue that's not really a clue."

"I'll try. There was a gorgeous painting over the bed. Would go lovely in my sitting room, if I still had one - a landscape of a lake.

An arch went into a huge wardrobe. Actually, I think they call it a dressing room. Every wall was lined with clothes and shoes and bags. I didn't go in, in case I was caught. There were some photos on her dressing table, and I looked out of the window and saw the gardener. He was talking to another man.

Then Charles came in to be seen. I'd never met the son before - a good-looking boy with bright red hair. We chatted for a bit while I was pinning the shirt, and he said he was studying architecture at Cambridge and was in his third year and what he wanted to do when he had finished, etc. He never asked about me, of course. But knowing me, I probably told him anyway. So he went off, and Angus came in, and I pinned him. Now Lord Amerston, which is his official title, is tall, dark, and handsome. He must have been the most eligible bachelor in Scotland when he was young. He's pretty hot now. As far as I can remember, he talked about the village's summer fayre that's on this weekend. Said how it cost a fortune to put on, and it would be cheaper if he just gave them the money they made for the charity in the first place. But it was expected of him. His family had been doing it for years, ever since it got too big to be held on the village green. I didn't like to say that I hadn't even been for two years. Poor man. It must be so hard to be Lord of the Manor," Abigail said sarcastically. "Then he said he needed to get some horses from the Pony Club for the pony rides, and did I fancy being a fortune teller as they hadn't found one yet? To which I declined naturally. I might have run a stall like the tombola or something if he'd have asked.

He said he was in no mad rush to have his golf trousers back as his wife had made sure he would have no time for fun anytime soon. He said it jokingly, but I think she is the boss, and he would much rather have been on the golf course and in the club drinking with his cronies rather than getting ready for the fayre. He thanked me, and I waited downstairs in the hall while he got changed. A maid came and asked me if I needed anything."

"Ooh, could it be the butler?" Betty suggested. "They say it always is, but I've never heard of one being guilty."

"They don't actually have one. There is a housekeeper, Mrs Bittens. But she's an old woman that's been there for years so I can't see it myself. We'll keep her on the list though, Betty. Then Helen joined me, and we chatted for a while about nothing in particular - family stuff probably. It was actually Charles that brought all the sewing down to me, and then I said goodbye and told her I would ring her when they were ready. And Charles collected them two days later. And he didn't give me a tip either. Tight git!"

Betty looked thoughtful. "Nothing that would lead to murder, is there? Who was the gardener talking to? Perhaps he was receiving stolen goods from the estate. Although I doubt it. I know old Arthur, and he wouldn't pinch so much as a rose from there. He told me he'd even asked permission if he could have a cutting of the virginia creeper for me. It never did take, incidentally. Maybe the painting was stolen from the Louvre. Or it's a forgery, and they sold the real one for an insurance claim."

"I think you're in the realms of fantasy now, Betty dear," said Lillian gently.

"So it's back to the ironing board then," she replied seriously. "Wasn't there anybody else?"

"It's hard to remember; it seems like a lifetime ago, but it is, I suppose. Hang on, I can't remember which day it was, but another of my richer customers booked an appointment for one evening. That was Nathan Hill. Now he's an accountant to some really famous and rich clients - footballers, actors. Maybe even the Hattons, come to think of it. So he turns up in his brand new Jaguar and parks outside. He had a Ralph Lauren suit to alter, so he went upstairs to change, and thinking about it, he could have noticed the detector up there. Ooh, now I remember, as I was doing the sleeves, his phone went. I'd forgotten about that."

"Do you know who it was?" asked Suzie, excitedly.

"Being me, I did just happen to see the screen, and it said someone named Ashwin. Hmmm...Andrew, I think. Nathan was a bit abrupt with him and said 'I told you, it's nothing whatsoever to do with me. I know two million is a lot... look, don't phone again.' And he cut the call off. Nathan rolled his eyes and said 'Sorry about that,' and that was that. Then he changed the subject and asked me what I had been up to."

"Now we're getting somewhere," said Betty. "A suspect at last."

Terry frowned and said, "Andrew Ashwin... I'm sure I've heard that name recently."

"Can't say I have," said Jim. "Think, Terry. Where would you have heard it?"

"It'll come to me in a sec. Ummm. I know where I saw it. Just before I met Abigail as I walked past the paper shop I saw it on the front page of the Chiltern Weekly. You're not going to believe this, folks. It said his body was found hanging in Ridgeway Woods!"

"Fantastic," Abigail shouted. "Not for him, of course, but you know what I mean. It's another lead to follow up."

"We need to read the paper and find out whatever we can," Terry said. He jumped to his feet to have a look for it. But Abigail had other ideas.

She opened her eyes wide and exclaimed, "I've got a better idea. If we get a move on, we might be able to speak to the man himself. Come on, let's go to Ridgeway Woods!"

Betty looked over at Terry and thought he wouldn't be at all pleased. As the one who had been there the longest, they all looked to him for advice. Abigail was taking over, and she had only just got there.

Terry was thinking the same thing. He used to be the one in charge, and now he was really regretting bringing this bossy woman into their gang. And the worst of it was that they seemed to be lapping it up. Oh well, they'll soon be bored of her. Although it was rather exciting, he had to admit.

Chapter 4

LUCKILY, THE WOODS WERE ON THE OUTSKIRTS OF Becklesfield, so they didn't have far to walk. Abigail and Lillian both said how much they missed not being able to jump in a car. Betty stayed with Suzie in the library because she did not think a hanging body was a good experience for a young girl. Not only that, Suzie was very good at turning the pages of a new magazine that had just arrived.

Terry, Jim, Lillian and Abigail joined the signposted footpath to Upper Belling, not that there was a Lower one. It went straight through the centre of the woods. Terry had been born in the nineteen-thirties and spent a great deal of his youth there, when there were no computer games and all the boys had penknives. He wasn't sure, but he didn't think they had them these days. He wondered how they would cut down the foliage now to build their dens. It was a whole different world now, he thought. But the ancient beech and oak trees stayed the same. The woods weren't that big, maybe five hundred acres, but it was still going to take a miracle to find Andrew Ashwin before darkness fell.

They were beginning to think that maybe he had departed

when Terry spotted a friend. To the side of the path, a lady dressed in Victorian clothes was sitting on a tree stump. On her lap was a wicker basket filled with bluebells.

"Good day to you, Rosie. May I introduce Lillian, Abigail, and Jim."

"Hello, Terry. What brings all of you round this neck of the woods? Could it be that you want to take another stroll with me?"

"What a lovely idea. I will take you up on that if you can tell us if you've seen a man wandering around here lately?"

"When did he arrive? There's a lot of men here, you know." As if to prove her point, a stocky young man carrying a chainsaw appeared from the undergrowth then passed straight through the trunk of a huge oak tree.

"Within the last week," said Abigail. "Possibly smartly-dressed. We don't actually know what he looks like."

"Smartly dressed, you say? Well, that makes a change. The men I see these days are a right scruffy lot. I never saw my Bill without his collar and cuffs on. And some of them are only wearing half trousers above the knees and showing their arms. Not even any socks and goodness knows what they are wearing on their feet. What happened to leather shoes and boots? I honestly have to avert my eyes sometimes. As for the ladies, we'd have got arrested for going out like that. An ankle was considered racy," she cackled. "Mind you, I could do without this corset on, that's for sure. But I suppose I'm an old relic."

"Not old. You'll never be old, Rosie."

"I lived to the grand old age of fifty-eight. That's older than anyone else in my family. I've heard people can live till they are eighty now, is that right?"

"My nan lived until she was one hundred and one and received a telegram from the queen," said Lillian.

"No? From Queen Victoria? Are you royalty or something?"

"Far from it, Rosie, and it was Queen Elizabeth."

"Heavens above. Now I've heard everything. I was one of ten children, and only four of us made old bones. Where were we? Oh yes, a smart man. Hmm. I did see one a couple of days ago. Found him hanging in the tree and him just looking up at himself in shock. He might still be there if you're quick."

Terry went over and gave her a hug. "You're an angel and a lady, Rosie. As soon as we've had a word, we'll come back and all have a walk with you. How's that?"

"How lovely. I'll wait right here. So follow the path and take the first right fork; that's where the body was, but that's gone now. He might be round and about though."

He hadn't gone far, and they found him faster than they thought they would. "Andrew Ashwin, I presume," shouted Terry.

"Thank God for that. I've never been so glad to see someone or rather someone see me. I've been wandering around these woods for days. How do you know my name?"

"You were in the paper." Terry introduced his friends and proceeded to tell him what he'd had to tell people for the last fifty years about where they were. Andrew had worked that much out for himself. The what, why, and when were not so clear.

"Have you heard of Nathan Hill? He's an accountant from Gorebridge."

"Yes, he's been a colleague for years. Funnily enough, I've been thinking of him ever since I came to. Is this his fault? I knew it. I never did like him and his smarmy ways."

"What do you remember about what happened?" asked Abigail.

"I know I had no money left and I borrowed a lot off someone I shouldn't have. Was it Nathan? I don't think so. But I can't be sure. I think I was going to lose my house and maybe even go to jail for five years. I keep picturing my wife and boys, and I can see their sad faces. The last thing I can think of is an oak tree above me and a rope. Did I kill myself? I'd like to think that I didn't, but I have no idea. Tell me I didn't."

"If you did, no one would blame you," said Abigail. "Through no fault of your own, probably after a tip from Nathan, you lost two million pounds, maybe not yours. I'm sorry to say, but I don't think it was suicide, Andrew. We're here because we think Nathan might have murdered me, so chances are he killed you too. Lillian is a nurse. Let her have a look at the injuries on your neck."

After an extensive check, Lillian said, "It's too hard to say for sure, but definitely suspicious, I'd say. Your best bet is to go and see your wife and children and say goodbye or be there for them. If we hear any more, we'll let you know." A dejected Andrew left them in the woods to carry on with the investigation.

"Well, Lillian?" asked Terry. "Suicide or murder?"

"Definitely suicide, I'm sorry to say. I didn't have the heart to tell him. He must be starting to think there would have been an alternative to what he did. The angle of the rope mark was consistent with hanging. Strangulation would have been straight around the neck. Poor man. He will find peace now at any rate, hopefully."

"So the accountant is off the list now, is he?" asked Jim.

Abigail and Lillian did not agree. "Not at all. If he had lost all that money for a client and driven him to suicide, that would not do his reputation any good. How far would he go to keep that quiet? He knew you heard him talking to Andrew, and then the next minute his death is all over the papers. Whether it is suicide or murder, it wouldn't look good for him in front of all his fancy clients."

"We need a Breather, as I call them, to help," said Terry. "We need someone living to get details that not even Suzie could get to and ask some questions. I know there are ones that can communicate with us, but I've never met one."

"Breather?" queried Abigail.

"It was either that or a Liver, and that just sounded wrong. Breather, and we are the Deads."

"Makes sense, I suppose. Mind you, then I could have said - what am I chopped liver?" Terry groaned but smiled. "So we've got Movers, Deads, and Breathers." Abigail grabbed his arm in excitement. "I know one, a real live Breather who just happens to be a bona fide medium. She's amazing. She gets loads of good reviews and results, and tomorrow we can pay her a visit. She lives in Becklesfield, thank goodness. How lucky is that? Boy, will she be shocked. And apart from being dead, this must be my lucky day, because I've just remembered that she's married to a policeman!"

They kept their promise to Rosie and were so glad that they did. She showed them a private glade, carpeted with bluebells just like the ones in her basket. When a family of deer and a pair of fox cubs with their parents entered, Abigail really thought she had died and gone to Heaven.

The following day was luckily sunny - not even ghosts like the rain. Abigail couldn't hide her excitement that morning in the library as she told them all about the customer of hers who just happened to be a psychic. She'd done sewing for her and was given a free reading when her own mother had died and was amazed at the detail that she had got correct. She somehow knew that her mum had grown up on a farm and her father had been waiting for her by a stile in Heaven. Abigail had visited the farm near Upper Farthing many times and had often climbed over that very stile. That her favourite colour was blue and that she would never wear green as it was unlucky wasn't quite so impressive, but still true. They'd become friends after that and often chatted on the phone or went for coffee. But the proof would only come when they went to see her, and she could hear if not see them. Or as Betty put it, in her own inimitable way, "The proof will be in the Christmas pudding."

Abigail was so excited for them to meet her. "Hayley Moon, well that's her professional name, actually it's Hayley Bennett, is amazing at what she does. Not only is she a psychic medium, she's into horoscopes and tarot cards. Mostly though, she communicates with a dead loved one for others. She can even give you a reading over the phone, but that probably won't work for us. Hand on heart, she isn't a fake, but I guess we'll soon find out. And luckily she lives close to here, in Church Lane."

Chapter 5

ABIGAIL RECOGNISED THE HOUSE IN THE ROW OF five, which were built relatively recently for Becklesfield, in the nineteen fifties. Hayley's was the one with the dreamcatcher and wind chimes hanging in the porch. What was the etiquette for visiting with a medium or anyone come to think of it, she wondered. Should she get Suzie to knock on the big knocker? No, she'd simply go in, but through the front door - she still had manners.

Hayley was sitting in her conservatory with her feet up and eyes closed. She was listening to some loud, restful music, perfect for meditation. A large white candle burned on the sideboard, surrounded by crystals of all shapes and colours.

"Hayley, can you hear me? ... No, she can't. What a shame. HAYLEY. Turn that row off, please, Suzie. Aah, that got her attention." Hayley sat up as the music had abruptly stopped, and then suddenly the candle went out. Very odd, she thought.

"Hayley, it's Abigail. Abigail Summers, the dressmaker."

"Hi, hun. I'll let you in." She walked quickly to the window and then the front door. She straightened her ankle-length skirt. She had counted them once, and she owned twenty-eight of them, in all patterns and colours. It was how she first met Abigail. She couldn't walk past a charity shop without looking for one. More often than not, they were the wrong size, and she would call on the services of the best dressmaker in Becklesfield to make them fit. "Where are you, hun?"

"I told you she'd hear me. We're here, behind you."

Hayley turned around and was totally confused. "Where? I see some mist."

"That's us. I died, Hayley. And we need your help. You don't know how pleased we are that you aren't a fake. I told them you were the best around."

"We? How many of you are there?"

"Only four. Meet Terry, Suzie, and Betty. So sorry to turn up like this. We're all new to the psychic world. We weren't sure how to make contact. But I've always thought the direct approach is best, so we just walked into your house, I'm afraid."

"I can see you all now. Well, I'm blowed. I've never had such a clear vision."

"Please sit down again, Hayley. You look like you've seen a ghost!"

They all gathered in the living room. Which tickled Abigail when she realised the irony of it.

"Just let me get a large glass of white wine, please. I'm used to my spirit guide and different relatives talking to me in my mind, but they don't usually turn up unannounced in my hall," admitted a very pale Hayley. She tucked her long, black hair behind her ears and flopped on the leather armchair. "I had no idea you were dead, Abi. It wasn't in the paper."

Don't rub it in thought Abigail. "I am so sorry I shocked you like that, but you're our only hope. You see I didn't just die, I was murdered."

"We're all investigating," butted in Suzie.

"I need to know, Hayley. We won't put you in any danger, we promise."

"I'm not sure what I can do. If I knew everything that went on I'd have won the lottery by now, or... I get it. It's not just me you want, is it? Could it be that you remember that I'm married to a policeman?"

"It never crossed my mind. I'd forgotten about that," lied Abigail. "But now you mention it!"

"It won't do you any good. Besides, Tom's only a constable, so he doesn't hold much sway with anyone. But carry on. Tell me what you know so far."

Terry took up the story. "She was poisoned by carbon monoxide by persons unknown at the minute. There's a few names in the pot. Her niece and nephew, Nathan Hill, the accountant and the Hattons of Chiltern Hall. But that's only because they are the only people she's mixed with lately."

"I know the Hattons slightly," exclaimed Hayley. "I was a fortune teller at the May Day Fayre a few years ago. I turned them down this year. Even if it was for a good cause."

"Please reconsider, Hayley. It would give you chance to have a bit of a snoop. You could keep your eyes, ears, and any other senses open. Lord Angus will be over the moon if you volunteer. Sorry about the pun. He still hasn't managed to find one. He even asked me, so he must be getting desperate. Please think about it.

Then there's Nathan Hill, the accountant. He's rich, gorgeous but decidedly dodgy. Now he knew the bloke that died in the woods - Andrew Ashwin."

"I did read about him. They think he hanged himself. I said a prayer for the poor man, and I do hope he's crossed over."

"No, he hasn't," she answered, to Hayley's amazement. Not that he hadn't, but because Abigail knew. She was learning more in one day than she had ever known.

"My nephew, Aaron, could have done it too. He's already taken over my house and doesn't seem a bit sorry that his only aunt died an awful death. Do you think Tom could help? It might be a feather in his cap if he catches a killer."

"He's not a detective, so I'm not sure how. But he's really good at what he does. Mainly because he's such a caring sort. But I don't think you'll have any joy with him because he doesn't believe in the supernatural at all. I try to keep it from him if I can, and if I start, he puts his hands over his ears and starts lalaing."

"Maybe we can prove to him that you're the real deal."

Hayley looked at her watch. "Well, you can try because he'll be home any minute."

Tom Bennett, the young, handsome police constable, worked out of the neighbouring town, Gorebridge. The crime rate was a lot higher than in his village, Becklesfield. After a long day arresting shoplifters and breaking up fights, the last thing he wanted to deal with was his wife's rubbish. He was hoping for a bottle of lager and a nice thick steak and chips, then feet up and television on till he nodded off. But she was really testing his patience tonight. He was only half listening. Something about a murder, a hanging, the May Day Fayre, and a dressmaker had been poisoned.

"Tom, I don't ask you for much." Hayley ignored the face he gave her. "All they want is for you to look at the files of Abigail Summers and Andrew Ashwin when you go in tomorrow. They both died recently in very suspicious circumstances."

That got his attention. "You've got to be kidding. Not only is it a waste of time, I could lose my job if I'm caught. I know your spirit guide told you where that little girl had run off to, but my boss said it was simply a good guess on your part."

"And I just happened to guess that the jewellery from that robbery was wrapped in a tablecloth and hidden in that barn, I suppose."

"Even then, Detective Chief Inspector Johnson said it was a coincidence. When I see proper proof, I'll believe you." Whereupon he picked up the remote control and turned the television on. But Suzie immediately pressed the red button to turn it off. That got his attention.

"Great. Now the TV's broken."

"Sorry, Abi. I knew he'd never go for it. Even if it would help with his career." Tom rolled his eyes at his wife talking to nobody. It wasn't the first time.

"Well, one thing we can do is give him proof of how good you really are, Hayley. Tell him the ghost of a little girl is about to push that photo frame off the windowsill."

"Tom, keep your eye on your nan's photo." Tom jumped up when it fell on the carpet.

"That could be the wind. Or on a bit of string. What else have you got?" said Tom.

"Pick up that book. Open any page and point to a word."

"Okay... This one."

"Dismal. Never. Chapter. The. Between," repeated Hayley after Abigail saw which word his finger was pointing to.

"Actually, that is pretty impressive, Hayley."

"Now do you believe me? It's not my spirit guide this time. Abigail is here, and she wants to know if her death is being investigated. It was put down to carbon monoxide poisoning. Probably accidental as there were no detectors in the house. But Abi knows for a fact that two had been removed. So if that isn't murder, I don't know what is!"

Tom looked like he had seen a ghost as well now. "I've got to think about it. I don't really want you getting involved. If there is a murderer about, what's to stop them from coming after you?"

"You know I've always thought my abilities were a special gift from God. If I don't put them to good use, what is the point? I need this, and there's got to be a reason that Abigail came to me. You give back to people with your job all the time, and I know I help those that have lost someone, but this is a real chance for me to prove to others, you and especially myself that I have got the gift. Please, Tom. I beg you."

"Okay, I give in. I'll have a look at the online files when I get in. I'll give you a ring in my break, but I'm not writing it down or bringing any files home. I don't want to leave a trail. I could get in serious trouble. Johnson would like nothing more than to get me the sack."

"At least you haven't got to be a fortune teller at the May Day Fayre on Saturday. I've got to give readings while getting them to talk. And I bet they make me wear that ridiculous red and gold get-up again. They've got a very funny idea of what us psychics wear. Still, it's a one-off, I don't suppose we'll have to help the spirits again, and it is for charity."

Everyone thanked Tom via Hayley, and Terry told her to come to Becklesfield Public Library at about three o'clock the next day to tell them what she had learned. Where should they meet? Hayley asked.

Where else? The True Crime Section!

Chapter 6

I<small>T WAS LIGHT THE NEXT TIME THAT</small> J<small>ESSICA WOKE</small>, and she realised that she was in an attic. Not a basement, thank God. She had seen far too many of those films to know that that never ended well. Her head still hurt, and she knew that she had been drugged. There was a small dormer window above her, and the sky was as dark as her future. This time she could take in her surroundings. In a way, she wished she couldn't. She didn't have the strength to get off the bed. She saw a big heavy door, and the walls were lined with boards, the kind her grandad had lined his shed with. Although he called it a man cave to get away from Nana.

It was an old metal bed she was on, like she thought. At least it had a fairly clean sheet and pillow on it, but the mattress had a horrible smell that she didn't even want to think about. Next to her was an old plastic bucket, the thought of which made her feel sick. She saw two bottles of water and some packets of crisps and plain, cheap biscuits. So, whoever had brought her here didn't want her to starve. They obviously didn't want her to die then, she thought as her eyes filled with tears. Jessica felt woozy again, and she wished she could pass out; actually, she wished she could die. But then a sudden anger took over her. Why should she die? No, the fight for her life was important. She refused to die here, where she might never be found.

She heard a sound and held her breath and sat bolt upright. Was that footsteps? Thud, thud, thud. Surely someone was coming closer? Her eyes were wider than they had ever been. Then the noise stopped. She breathed out, her chest tight as a drum. Jessica had only lived in modern houses, so she wasn't prepared for the creaking and groaning of a house that age, which came to life with the changes of temperature and the wind. Her body gave a shudder and relaxed. No one there, she told herself. No one there.

She opened the water. Her thirst was excruciating; she couldn't stand it any longer. It went through her mind that it might be drugged, but she needed it. Jessica had heard somewhere that you can go without food for a long time, but not water. She only drank half of the small bottle as it crossed her mind that she might be there for a long time, and it would have to last. Oh, that tasted so good. She swirled the liquid around her mouth and savoured every bit of it. Four mouthfuls would have to do for now.

The only other bit of furniture in the room was a pine chair. Was he going to sit on it? Her stomach dropped at the thought. Her favourite blue coat, which she always wore when she went out anywhere special, was over the back. Maybe she could balance it on the bed and look out of the window or climb out of it, but she didn't think she would be able to fit through. The sight of her coat caused a few flashbacks. Jessica could remember putting it on. But where was she going? Visions of a smiling man with a beard appeared in her mind's eye. In a pub, maybe. A date of some sort? He looked a lot older than her usual boyfriends. Had she met him online? It suddenly came to her, his name was Robin! We had arranged to meet at the pub - The Greyhound, she remembered. I got the bus there. He seemed friendly enough. A nice smile. She felt a bit sick and tried to get up to see if the door was open, but fell back. She would have to look out of the window later. Dizziness came again, and her eyelids got heavy. She was passing out, so escape would have to wait. She had been right; there was something in the water. Damn.

Chapter 7

JUST BEFORE THREE O'CLOCK ON THE THURSDAY afternoon, Hayley proudly walked into the library. All the stick she'd received from all those non-believers over the years had gone through her mind. From the ones accusing her of taking advantage of the bereaved to others saying she was just good at guessing. Who cares anymore? If they didn't want to believe, that was their loss. Even before Abigail, she knew the gift she had was God-given. But she was so happy that Tom didn't have any more doubts. Seeing really was believing. He had proved it by telling Hayley what he had found out. He didn't write anything down for her and told her not to either, so she just hoped she could remember all he had said. He daren't risk it getting into the wrong hands. DCI Johnson wasn't that keen on the young, popular bobby who had the look of someone who was going to make it to CID and probably go higher than him.

They all gathered around her when they saw her entering the library.

"Come and sit down, Hayley," said Betty. "This is Lillian and Jim. They're helping us to investigate as well."

"Hello, nice to meet you. I better tell you what I've learned very quickly. Tom wouldn't let me write anything down or text it in case he was found out. He could get in real trouble if he was found to be giving information to anyone, even if they were deceased," she laughed. "So right, listen carefully. Don't interrupt as it will put me off, Abigail. I know what you're like.

Now your boiler flue must have been blocked for at least two days, hun. Which was strange as an engineer had inspected it, as you know, six weeks ago. It was blocked outside with twigs and leaves to give the impression that a bird had made a nest. But you don't have to be David Attenborough to know that it's the wrong time of year. The pressure was on full as well, so it was an accident waiting to happen.

Gwen Giles, your next-door neighbour, can remember seeing a workman in a cap and overalls going up your path on one of the days. And there might have been a white van up the road, but that could have been any time. They knew something was wrong when Brooks Boutique didn't get their customers' alterations back. You were always punctual and had never let them down. You were found in your bed with no other signs of injury. DCI Johnson noticed there was no detector, and there was a screw with nothing on it in the kitchen, but he put it down to Abigail being a female and therefore not realising. His words, not mine or Tom's. Your nephew and niece were given permission to move in, as they had recently been thrown out of a rental house because the owner wanted to sell. Also, they are your official next of kin and have a key, so they didn't think it would be a problem. And it was better than being empty and an attraction for burglars. They didn't have an alibi for the previous days, apart from each other. No other inquiries will happen till after the inquest. But the investigators have just put it down to accidental death and you not taking enough precautions."

Abigail was almost bursting, trying to give her side, but she managed to keep quiet like Hayley wanted.

"This is what was in the Andrew Ashwin file. Basically, he

was found hanging from a tree in Ridgeway Woods. His inquest has not been held yet, but all signs point to suicide as he was deeply in debt and had lost a lot of money for his financial firm. There was no suicide note. Although I am going to tell his wife to look on the fridge door. Would you believe I've had a vision that Aiden, his little boy, drew a dinosaur on the back for his mother, and she put it under a fridge magnet? I think that's all. He was found by an elderly couple walking their dog. I just hope I haven't forgotten anything."

"Well done on remembering all that, Hayley. And that's amazing that you know where the suicide note is. It could have just got screwed up and thrown away. At least his poor wife will know why. The fact that it's about money and nothing to do with her must help."

"Thank you, Betty. I don't know whether to go round there or send a letter. I've visited families before, and they just assume I'm there because I want money for it. What happened to people doing something for nothing? I think I'll send a condolence card and write it in there. I might put my number or my website on there in case she wants to get in touch."

"I didn't know you had a website, Hayley," said Abigail.

"Of course. Most mediums do. I offer readings or angel card advice. Links to all things spiritual and meditation, CDs, dream analysis etc. I actually do faith healing, but I suspect I'm a little on the late side for any of you. Sorry, I shouldn't joke."

"Don't worry about it," said Terry. "It's how we get through the days. I have a feeling if you solve this, you'll be famous."

"You might get a virus."

"I think you mean go viral, Betty," said Lillian.

"More than likely," said Betty. "We barely had electricity when I was born, so I need to catch up on these new-fangled words."

"Actually, I'd rather Tom get the credit. My phone will be ringing non-stop else. Hopefully, I'll get a few more clients though. Plus, there will be the usual trolls that tell me I'm a nutcase."

Luckily for her, neither she nor the ghosts had seen all the funny looks this nutcase was getting, giving a speech to herself. Some of the patrons and the librarian thought it was a shame that she was out without her carer and there really should be more help available for people like her.

"From what it says in my file, I don't think they will be doing anything about it any time soon. I'm an accident, and poor old Andrew was a suicide. Even if he was, there was someone else responsible. It's up to us to find the proof, I guess."

"We're ready," said Terry and the others all agreed.

"We'll start with the Hattons on Saturday then. Hayley will talk to whoever she can while using her crystal ball, and we'll do a little bit of breaking and entering, or actually when I think of it, entering!"

Friday was spent in the library, planning their next strategy and just relaxing as well. Abigail knew tiredness was no longer an issue, but it was still nice to just take in her new life, if she could call it that. The weather was chilly, and it poured with rain, but luckily, on the day of the May Day Fayre at Chiltern Hall, the sun was shining without a cloud in the sky. For the first time, Abigail wished she could have put on some sandals and a floaty, flowery dress. Pyjamas did not go with the special outdoor occasion in the sunshine. All of them had decided to go to the fayre, and Suzie was so excited that Lillian and Jim had a job to keep up with her.

It really was a marvellous sight and looked as it would have done many years ago. Bunting of all different colours was tied to every marquee and side show. The coconut shy was using the same wooden posts and balls that Terry had thrown over sixty years before. Suzie went to the hoopla and threw a hoop over a goldfish bowl, much to the surprise of the stallholder. Lillian and Jim said they would take her to have a ride on the ponies next.

Abigail, Terry, and Betty made their way to an open-fronted tent with a sign proclaiming 'The Marvellous Hayley Moon - World Famous Fortune Teller to the Stars'.

"How's it going?" asked Terry.

"Ooh, you made me jump," said Hayley, who was wearing the red and gold gypsy outfit. She had refused to wear the headscarf; her waist-long hair looked the part anyway.

"You never foresaw that then," said Betty, jokingly.

"Haha. It's been okay. I've seen two teenagers so far. Just told them what they all want to hear. Fame on the TV and loads of boyfriends. I don't want to get too serious in my predictions; they only come in for a bit of fun, and I'm only doing this for you. Here's all I know so far. Helen is the welcoming committee, and Angus is helping on the stalls. I'm hoping to give them a reading and find out some more information. Charles seems to be permanently in the beer tent so far. I saw him drinking with the Morris Dancers. I think they are getting Dutch courage for when they do their bit later on. Why don't you go and look at the Maypole Dance? It's just about to start. It's quite a spectacle if you've never seen it."

"Good idea. Don't forget to ask loads of questions to the punters and try and find out what the Hattons have been up to. See you later." Abigail led them out of the tent, and they went to join the spectators.

They were just in time to see the Mayor crown the May Day Queen. She was announced as thirteen-year-old Layla Kaye from the local school. She was wearing a white dress trimmed with pale pink, and now she had a garland crown of yellow, red, and pink flowers on top of her long blonde hair. The Mayor then introduced the twelve children from the Becklesfield Primary School who had been practising for a month how to dance around the sixteen-foot maypole. It was the same one that had been in use for over a hundred years. The six boys and six girls held a ribbon that was attached to the top that were all the colours of the rainbow. As the local band started to play, they began to skip and weave in and out of each other. By the time the music had stopped, the pole was adorned with a perfect pattern of ribbons. Abigail, Terry, and Betty stayed to join in the applause and then walked through the rest of the festivities. They saw Charles with all his mates enjoying a beer, including the Morris Dancers resplendent in their white and red costumes. Abigail was surprised to see that Aaron and Monica were in the craft marquee, so she went in to see what they were up to. They were browsing at the homemade cake stall and bought some pieces at the Bric-A-Brac.

"And they had the cheek to throw my stuff out, and they've just bought a china carthorse from the eighties and a teapot in the shape of an elephant. Seriously, what are they thinking? I find it hard to believe we are even related. Come on, let's go in the house and do some sleuthing. The good thing is, we can't get caught, or can we? I wonder if we will show up if they've got surveillance cameras, Terry?"

"Actually, I do know about that. Sometimes we set them off, but we just come out as orbs. Or sometimes as a black shadow. Same with normal cameras."

"How exciting. I hope my nephew gets one put in. I'll keep setting it off. But I doubt he will. He'll know with stuff like that teapot and carthorse, they won't get too many burglars! That reminds me, come on."

Chiltern Hall was a classic example of a Georgian building. The facade was perfectly symmetrical even down to the windows, the chimney pots, and the trees on either side. They climbed the central white, stone steps to the grand entrance, and Abigail wasn't at all surprised that there were exactly ten. She loved symmetry herself and worked it into all her designs.

"I feel like we ought to go in the tradesman's entrance," said Terry jokingly.

"At least they never made me do that," answered Abigail as they walked through the heavy oak door and into the hall. The housekeeper, old Mrs Bittens, was coming down the grand staircase carrying a basket of laundry. Didn't even give her the day off, they all thought. When she reached the three of them, she shivered.

Abigail turned to Terry. "So it's true then, the temperature drops when we're around?"

"Usually. Don't ask me why."

"Remind me to go round to Aaron's on a cold day! Come on, much as I would love to be nosy and see the rest of the house, we'd better get upstairs."

At first sight, the master bedroom looked exactly the same. The oil painting over the bed was even nicer than Abigail remembered, but perhaps she just appreciated the good things in life more now. It was of a sailing boat on a lake. But as she looked more closely, she realised it was a loch in Scotland going by the landscape around it. Maybe it was near the stately home they owned up there.

"Oh my giddy aunt," exclaimed Betty. "Just look at all those clothes. There's more in that cupboard than me and my John had all our lives. We had one pair of outdoor shoes and one comfy pair; why on earth does she need twenty pairs? You can still only wear one pair at a time. What a waste of money."

"How the other half live, eh, Betty."

Terry was looking at the photographs on the dressing table that Abigail had talked about. The biggest one was of Lady Helen sitting on the back of a sailing boat. She had a cap on and was looking into the distance. It could have been taken anywhere, but might have been on that loch, thought Abigail. A photograph of a family of four, in an ornate silver frame was next to it. By the look of it, the photo had been taken in the seventies, going by the long-haired man with his huge, pointed collar. Whoever he was, and it was probably Angus' dad, his purple and orange tie was about four inches wide. It was taken in the doorway of a church. Perhaps guests at a wedding as the man and woman both had rosebuds on their left side. The man carried a baby of about six months, smiling away with a mass of dark curls. A red-haired little boy was holding his mother's hand. "That's so sad," said Abigail. "I forgot about that. Angus had a brother, Graham, and he died young. They all looked so happy there."

The last one was a shooting party of three people and a Jack Russell. Scotland they supposed, as there was heather and hills in the background. One of them looked like a younger Angus. An older one that looked like the man in the church photograph, so probably his father, was standing next to him. A chap with blue eyes and ginger hair was on the end and holding up a pheasant. He was about fifty, so not Angus' brother. He had a beautiful smile, which made Abigail feel sad momentarily. She'd never again flirt or simply fancy someone again. She had found in her short life that it was more important to like someone than they like you. The trick was to find feelings that were mutual. She had never quite succeeded in that. There was one bloke, when she was in her twenties that was always asking her to get engaged and the one she would have married in a heartbeat and had six children with, treated her more like a friend. Perhaps she was better out of the dating game. She always lost. Abigail came out of her daydream when Betty spoke.

"Come on, you all must be thinking it. Red hair! Now Charles has red hair. Could that be the reason? This is his real dad. And he's a family friend or even the gamekeeper. A real-life Mellors. Naughty Helen."

"We'd better not start that rumour just yet," added Abigail. "And it seems a bit drastic to murder me over that."

"You're joking. This is hereditary peerages we're talking about. It hasn't changed for hundreds of years. Women still can't inherit a title and estate if there is an older brother. Charles might not be able to inherit if his dad is not the Lord but this chap is," said Terry. "But why keep the photo? Surely they wouldn't want his picture where anyone could see it. And I'm sure Angus would have had an inkling that the bloke there could be Charles' dad and not him."

"Not necessarily, and most people wouldn't get to see it. I usually do the pinning in the spare room where the big mirror is. The only reason I came in here that day was to give Helen a quote for the curtains. The man next to Angus could just be a friend. I think we can presume that the older one is the last Lord Hatton, or rather Lord Amerston, because he's in the other one at the church."

"Maybe Helen is or was in love with the man with red hair, and it was the only picture she had of him. And poor Angus might not even know that Charles isn't his son," said Betty. "I think it could easily be a motive for murder, but I can't think why you, for the life of me. Let's hope the Marvellous Hayley Moon is having more luck."

Chapter 8

"FIVE POUNDS, PLEASE, LADY HELEN."

"Of course. I don't expect special treatment." Although she sounded like she was hoping for it. She pushed her sunglasses back on her head and sat down at the table opposite Hayley.

"You look lovely. The dress is gorgeous and fits you so well. I must be a funny shape, short-bodied or something. I can never get anything to fit. That's why I always wear long skirts," said Hayley, hoping she would take the bait.

"I have most of my clothes fitted. A lady called Abigail altered it for me. Unfortunately, she recently died. Such a shame. I will miss her dreadfully."

"Oh, I'm so sorry."

"Yes, good dressmakers are so hard to find." Hayley thought she'd better not relay that part of the conversation. So she started with the fortune telling.

She held her hands over the crystal ball and moved them around. It wasn't hers, but had been in the prop box for the last fayre, so she had no idea how it worked. She shut her eyes and allowed her thoughts to come to the fore. "There's a big change coming in the near future. I see a boat trip."

ANN PARKER

"We've got a boat," exclaimed Helen. "Hopefully it will be a cruise, though. I'm not that keen on the water."

Hayley carried on for a while telling her what she was feeling but also telling her what she wanted to hear. "There will be a new addition to your family that will make a difference to your life. But I sense you are exhausted and you need to take some time off for yourself and get away."

"You don't know the half of it, Hayley. We've had a meeting every day for the last two weeks. Although we did have a bit of a break. The three of us went up to Scotland, to Amerston, the main estate last Wednesday for two nights." That's annoying, thought Hayley. Did that mean they had an alibi for the time that Abigail's house was broken into and the boiler was sabotaged?

"It was the twentieth anniversary of the death of Angus' young brother, Graham. We met up with his daughter, Caroline, to visit his grave. He and his wife both died in a boating accident. It was such an awful tragedy. She lived with us after that. Her and Charles are more like brother and sister. Now she's living in London, trying to earn her living as an actress."

"I have a feeling she will be very famous one day. Would I have seen her in anything?"

Helen shrugged. "She's been in a few unknown plays but nothing major. She is a lovely girl, though. We are all very fond of her."

"Is she coming today, or is she still in Scotland?" asked Hayley.

"No, she left when we did but I don't think she'll come. She prefers London. And she will probably be on stage tonight, being Saturday. I dare say she needs the money. It costs an awful lot to rent a flat in London."

Hayley couldn't help but feel that the Hattons were not good at sharing their money. Their own son, Charles, lived in the lap of luxury while his cousin struggled. Did Caroline have a reason to be bitter and was trying to frame her rich relatives? But what had that got to do with Abigail? Nothing was the answer - probably.

"So what happened to that dressmaker of yours, Alison, was it?"

"Abigail. I'm not really sure. She didn't look ill. But then sometimes one doesn't. Angus heard it from one of the staff. I think it was Mrs Bittens, the housekeeper. Luckily she had already altered this dress, or else I dread to think what I would have done. Why do you ask?" Helen said suspiciously.

"Oh no reason. I felt someone with the name A was trying to contact me," she lied.

"Well, if she does, could you ask her to recommend someone to do my alterations?" Hayley wasn't sure she was even joking. She certainly didn't seem concerned that she was going to be accused of her murder if Abigail was present. Unless acting ran in her family.

Hayley felt she wasn't going to get any more information from Lady Helen, so decided to try and find Lord Angus. She put up the sign 'Gone to the other Realm. Back soon'.

Angus was judging The Scruffiest Scruffy Dog Competition. They all looked quite mangy to Hayley but they were the best sort. A long-haired Jack Russell with short legs, huge ears, and a wagging, wonky tail was the winner. She went over to scratch him behind his ample ears.

"A good choice, Angus."

"I've had five Jack Russells. All mad, but loyal. I've always thought if they were the same size as an Alsation, we'd all be in trouble. How did the fortune telling go?"

"I've taken over £50 so far. It's gone a bit quiet now, so I thought I'd have a break. Lady Helen said you had a trip to Scotland last week. I love Edinburgh. Were you anywhere near there?"

"No, we weren't. The estate I took over when my father died, oh, a couple of decades ago, is in the Highlands. A beautiful place - Amerston Manor. It's very isolated so we prefer to spend more time here. Although Christmas and New Year it's the best place in the world to be. We had to cut the trip short to get back for the fayre. There's always some committee or other to sit on. I wanted to stay for a round of golf but wasn't allowed by the boss - she who must be obeyed. We just stayed the two nights. Charles stayed an extra night. He had an assignation with a young lady or a Young Farmer's do. I wasn't really listening. We had to get back to make sure the grounds were all ready. Arthur, our gardener, is getting a bit long in the tooth, so we hired a couple of young lads to give him a hand. Anyway, if you'll excuse me, it's now time for the Scarecrow Competition. There's no rest for the wicked." How wicked? Helen was wondering.

A woman came over and whispered something in his ear. Angus frowned. "Excuse me, Hayley, unfortunately there's a little boy missing. I've got to make an announcement on the tannoy. Do have a look around. The gardens are beautiful this time of year."

"Please let me know if there's anything I can do. My husband is on duty at the gate; do you want me to find him?"

"No, thank you. I'll see to everything. I've got plenty of stewards here today, so I'm sure we can find him."

Hayley decided to take his advice and look around the gardens. He was right; they were beautiful. What was that saying about being nearer to God in a garden than anywhere else?

. . .

Abigail, Betty, and Terry heard about the missing child while they were looking for Hayley. "We have a lost child announcement. Please look out for Dexter Davis, aged 6. He's wearing a red t-shirt and blue shorts. If you find him, please bring him to the main tent. Thank you."

"Those poor parents," said Betty. "I lost one of mine at the seaside once, and it was the worst fifteen minutes of my life. And things were not so dangerous back then. He'd just wandered off and couldn't see us on the beach. Even he was terrified. We've got to help. Maybe we can go places they can't."

"Good idea, Betty," said Abigail. Terry said he'd go and have a look by the river. Water was always a magnet for children. He just hoped he wouldn't be talking to little Dexter in the flesh, so to speak, anytime soon.

There were two boys on the riverbank, but Terry could see straight away that neither of them was the toddler. They looked to be about twelve or so and were dressed in clothes from a century ago. With them was a woman from later years, wearing navy trousers and white trainers. They were standing on the bank by a small wooden building - a summerhouse of sorts, he imagined.

"Can you see us?" the lady asked. This was usually the first thing they said to him.

"Yes, I can see you all. I'm Terry. Is there anything I can do for you?"

"How nice to meet you, Terry. I'm Georgina, and this is Albert and Lenny. If you can tell us where these poor boys' parents are, we would really appreciate it."

"I'm afraid not. In fact, I'm looking for someone myself. A little boy of six called Dexter has gone missing. I don't suppose you've seen him, have you?"

"No, I haven't. What about you, boys? Have you seen Dexter around here?"

The taller one answered. "Seen lots of families, but not a

young'un on his own. We would have stopped him. Knowing what we know now. Lenny fell in, and I tried to save him. I couldn't."

"I'm so sorry, boys. How long have you been here?"

"Dunno. A long time."

"Would you like help to move on? I know someone who could help if you wanted."

Georgina answered for all of them. "No thank you, Terry. We'll wait a bit longer to see if anyone comes for the boys. I don't suppose you have seen my daughter, have you? She's about five, but might be a bit older now. I can't go without seeing her for the last time."

"Not that I know of, but I will keep an eye out."

"Thank you. We are alright, you know. It's a lovely spot, so don't worry about us. We'll keep an eye out for your little boy. Lenny and Albert will stop him if he gets too near the water. Please visit again, Terry. It can get a bit lonely."

Terry promised that he would and left them sitting on the riverbank. As much as he would have liked to, he couldn't help everybody. He carried on walking downstream, but Dexter was nowhere in sight. Once he got to the bend in the river, he turned back and went to find the others.

Betty and Abigail looked at the children proudly showing their scarecrows to the judges but couldn't see him anywhere. Every time they saw a small head, they rushed over, but not one of them was Dexter.

They caught sight of Suzie who was still with the ponies. She was stroking the smallest one's neck, and he was loving the attention. From the way he was nuzzling up to her, it was obvious he could see her.

Abigail called out to her. "Suzie, have you seen a little boy about? He's got on a red top and blue shorts."

"He was here earlier. Got too close to the ponies, so his mum told him to come away. Last I saw, he was over there by the bales of hay. He was trying to climb them. I don't know where he went after that."

"You're younger than us, climb up and see if he fell behind them or something, please."

They were delighted when Suzie told them that Dexter Davis was curled up on the top of the bales having his lunchtime nap, without a care in the world. They all split up to go and find Hayley. Betty was so pleased when she eventually found her by the fountain. "Hayley, great news, we've found the missing boy. Pretend you've had a vision or something. He's by the horses on top of the hay bales."

"That's fantastic, even I was starting to worry. In a way, I suppose I am doing this spiritually. But I can't help feeling a bit of a cheat while you do all the work. I tell you what, Tom's on duty by the gate. I'll give him a call. I expect he's already looking for him anyway."

Five minutes later, Constable Tom Bennett was a hero for saving the day. An announcement was made on the loudspeaker by Lord Angus. The parents and the Hattons couldn't thank him enough. Perhaps this supernatural stuff was not that bad, thought the young policeman.

Once Betty had returned with Hayley, the investigators sat on the grass in the sun, and they brought each other up to date on what they had found out. Hayley told the others what she had learned from the Hattons and the fact that they all had an alibi on the crucial days. Of course, Tom would have to check with the staff at Amerston Manor and with Charles' cousin, Caroline, but she had a feeling that they really were in Scotland.

"Now, Caroline is a Hatton, but she definitely isn't rich like they are. They don't seem to be supporting her either, even though her parents are both dead."

Abigail agreed. "I said exactly that. They're definitely on the cheap side. I never got a tip from them once. One time I did a job for her on the same day because she was going to Royal Ascot but not one penny extra. It was my fault though, I should have charged her double."

"That's why the rich are rich; they never give money out nilly willy." Betty pointed out as the others smiled.

They in turn told Hayley what they had seen in the bedroom and the red-haired theory, but they were finding it hard to find a motive. They described the picture of the boat and the one at the church. Betty told her about the painting and her idea of an art theft. But it all seemed a bit ridiculous as they were saying it. Perhaps it was simply Aaron and Monica. That made much more sense. Greed was the most likely motive; they all agreed. Betty said she should follow Nathan Hill around for a while. "He sounds a bit of alright!"

Hayley laughed. "At your age, Betty. Listen, why don't I pay him a visit on Monday? I could say I want to make an invest-ment or want to write a will or something."

Abigail thought it was a great idea. "Say you've been left some money by an aunt or something and you want to make some interest on it. He's got a posh office in Gorebridge."

"If he is guilty of your murder and even Andrew's, be careful of what you say. We don't want another death," urged Terry.

"I will, don't worry. And I won't tell Tom either. He'd kill me too. I think I ought to pay a visit to Aaron as well."

Abigail frowned. "Why don't you go when he is at work and see Monica when she's on her own? She's more likely to be interested in the paranormal, and no doubt she'd enjoy a free reading. You might be able to pick up on something. I could meet you there if you like."

Hayley shook her head and laughed. "Definitely not. All I would pick up on is your hatred of her. And you would never be able to keep quiet long enough for me to talk to her, let alone gauge her true feelings. Sorry, hun."

"You're probably right; I'd never be able to keep my mouth shut, and I am slightly biassed, I suppose." Abigail was starting to doubt herself. It still could be literally anyone. She was almost starting to wonder if she had taken the alarms off because they needed batteries. And did even the birds have it in for her and made a nest to finish her off? No. She could picture the detectors hanging there. She remembered thinking she should really wipe the one down that was at the top of the stairs. Housework was always 'I'll do that tomorrow.' No more tomorrows now. Oh well, no more dusting and hoovering. The Hattons could have hired someone, but would they want the chance that they could be blackmailed? Angus was a magistrate, so he could definitely have met the right kind of person. He could have let him off as a payment even. But she just didn't see it. And Hayley herself did not get the feeling that she had encountered a murderer when she'd been talking to them.

Abigail sighed and got to her feet. "I've had enough of this. We've reached a dead end - literally, actually. Let's enjoy the day while we're here. The Morris Dancers are starting soon. I do appreciate you all helping me. But we need to forget about me for a while." Terry thought that would make a change indeed. "And I promised Jim I would help him find out who stabbed him. Do you know where he lived, Terry?"

"No, I'm afraid not. But it's a good idea. I've been thinking his dead body might be lying there."

"I know where it is," said Betty. "He said he lived in a flat overlooking the park. Number ten, I think. Shall we go and get him? Where is he, does anyone know?"

Suzie gave a giggle. "I do. He's with Lillian, and they were getting all giggly and friendly. I think they're falling in love."

"Is that even possible?" asked Abigail with renewed hope. Maybe she would be able to play the dating game again. At her age, it used to be that all the good ones were married, and now, knowing her luck, all the good ones had crossed over.

"I don't see why not," answered Betty.

"Let's leave the two lovebirds to it then. At least we have a plan now. On Monday, me, Suzie, and Terry will go to Jim's flat to have a look around. Not Jim, though, just in case Terry is right, and his body is there. I don't think we should even tell him we're going. And Hayley will go and see Nathan Hill and Monica. Then we'll all meet at the library in the afternoon to see what we have found out."

Hayley rose as well. "I'm going back to do my bit for charity," she said. "Keep me posted, please. See you all later. Wish me luck. I sense The Marvellous Hayley Moon is going to be very busy!"

Chapter 9

JESSICA WOKE UP FOR THE THIRD TIME. THIS TIME SHE had no choice but to use the bucket. She had no idea how long she had been slipping in and out of consciousness. Now she was feeling fewer signs of being drugged, it was the hunger that was making her feel woozy, so she decided to have one of the biscuits. They were in a sealed packet, so hopefully, there were no drugs in them. She made a pledge to not drink the water. She needed to get her head together, however thirsty she got. If there was a chance to escape, she had to take it. The sky was a lovely blue now. Did that mean it was another day, or had the weather got better? How long had she been there? She was supposed to be going to the fayre at the hall at the weekend. Was that today, she wondered?

First thing she wanted to do was to check the door. She moved one leg slowly over the edge of the bed and lowered it to the ground. The metal frame creaked, and she stopped abruptly, but she needed to try to get out of there before someone came back. She still had her boots on, so she took them off and crept to the door. There was no carpet, only old floorboards, and she didn't want to make a noise in case someone was listening down below for her to come round. Her heart was thumping as she slowly turned the brass knob. It squeaked, and she stopped for a second. It was only when she realised that it was not opening that she forgot to be quiet and started banging on the door. "Let me out. Someone help me." An order at first but then a plea as the tears began to fall. Jessica had never been claustrophobic in her life, but the walls seemed to be closing in on her. She felt around them in case there was a weakness, but it all felt solid.

The next thing she did was stand on the bed to try and reach the little window. She could just touch it with her fingertips, so she went and got the wooden chair. It was very wobbly, but she managed to balance and steady herself on the ceiling. It was nailed shut and looked like it hadn't been opened for years, if ever. Many layers of paint had sealed her fate as well. From that angle, all she could see was the top of some trees to her left. She tried to hear something. Nothing. Where she lived, it was never this quiet. Even in the night, you could hear traffic. She had the chilling thought that she was in the middle of nowhere.

Now that Jessica was thinking a bit more clearly than before, she lay back down and tried to concentrate on what had happened at the pub. Yes, his name was Robin. She had thought that he must be nice with a name like that. She loved robins. She had been talking to him for a while online. Who suggested meeting at the Greyhound, she couldn't think, but off she had gone. He'd bought her a prosecco, that much she remembered, but then what? She had a feeling she had told him that she worked in an office, taking holiday caravan park bookings over the phone. He'd asked if she got a discount. He had said in his emails he ran his own business. What was it now? He told me at the pub. What the hell was it, again? Oh my God, she remembered, he did pest control. He caught rats, mice, and squirrels. Not just caught them, he killed them. It sounded like he enjoyed his job a bit too much. On a weekend, he spent the night at a friend's farm shooting foxes with his shotgun. They were vicious killers, he had said, as they attacked the livestock. It was about then she had started to get serial killer vibes. What the hell was she doing with him? She had two cats and gave to three animal charities every month. How could she get out of this? It had been very awkward all of a sudden. Is that when he kidnapped her?

She didn't think it was. In fact, she didn't have to worry. He had been the one to call it a night and said he had to go. She thought at the time bloody cheek. But she was so glad when he went.

So it wasn't him. A sort of blessing, she supposed. He had offered her a lift home. But had she accepted? Damn. She couldn't think. It must have been him. But no, she hadn't. She thought at the time, there's no way I'm getting in a car with him. She'd seen him walk out the door from the back, and she was still sitting in her chair. He even turned to give her a wave goodbye. Oh yes, it was then that she had noticed the hot guy by the bar.

How could she have forgotten him? He had turned and saw her staring. The pub was full, so he came over to sit on the only vacant chair. She couldn't believe her luck. He had a really expensive-looking suit on, cut to perfection. And brown shiny shoes. He'd made sure that his large gold Rolex watch was on show. Mum would have loved him on sight. Even his name was posh - Miles. And such a nice accent. He worked in London - in finance, he had said. He had that kind of floppy, untidy haircut that cost a fortune and a lot of time to do. Probably drives a Mercedes, she reckoned. She had started imagining introducing him to her friends. Even her parents this time. They'd be well impressed. 'That will show Auntie Tracy,' they'd say. The most perfect man ever! He drank G & T, of course. What was it he had said? 'I used to drink champagne, but I had a really bad hangover after an office party. So now I stick to gin or cocktails. And you're not supposed to get a hangover with champers, but I did.' Then he said to try one.

He had walked over to the table with two large glasses of gin and tonic in his hand, she remembered that. Her hand shook slightly as she raised the glass to her lips. He was staring to see if she liked it. Or to make sure she had some, with hindsight. Lovely, she'd said. The fact it was a bit bitter, she kept to herself and thought she'd rather stick to her prosecco, thank you very much. Maybe it was the lime she saw floating in it, she thought. She might try one with just ice next time. Yuck, it tasted awful. What had happened after that? It was a bit hazy. His arm around her shoulders - holding her up. A car ride? Why was I lying down though. That was her last memory. Looking up as the bright lights of the lampposts flashed by. "Idiot. How many times have I been told not to take drinks in case they're spiked! I've warned people myself, for God's sake. Just because he looked like he had money and was gorgeous, it went out the window. The bastard. I would have been better off with Robin. I ought to apologise to him. Never judge a book Mum had always said."

She tried to work out if anyone would miss her and call the police. Jessica shared a house with four other girls about her age. They would assume she'd gone to her mum's. Her mum would think she just hadn't phoned as usual. 'You never ring to see how your dad is. Your sister calls every day.' Well, Holly never rings me, so she's no good.

"Of course, they know," she told herself out loud. Actually, she'd be all over the papers and news - front page and on TV. Famous by now. 'Jessica Green has been abducted. Please look out for the pretty brunette, aged 22. Last seen wearing a blue coat with a good-looking man dressed in a grey suit and brown shoes, at a pub in the Becklesfield area. A reward is offered.'

They'd probably all want to interview her when they found her. "If they find me. I might lie here for all eternity, and not only that, they might think I had just run away, like I did when I was twelve." She couldn't just sit there, so she looked around. She was pleased to find a light switch as she had no idea of the time, and it might be dark soon. Jessica needed the light, not only as it was a hundred times scarier in the dark, but also someone might see it as they drove past. Just because she hadn't heard a car didn't mean there was no one about.

"Think, Jessica, what else can I do?" She was frightened of what her kidnapper might say, but she decided to smash the window. It was too small for her to get out of, but someone might hear her shout. Also, a neighbour might think there had been a break-in. She tried to break it by throwing a boot at it. But that just bounced off. The chair worked though. Straight through. Unfortunately, it put glass all over the bed. She was on a mission now. She'd be ready for him. She found the two biggest, deadliest shards of glass and put them under her pillow. That would make for a good interview on the BBC morning news. She took her coat and brushed the rest of the glass against the wall and on the floor so he wouldn't see it. She lay back exhausted but slightly more optimistic. Then she had an idea to throw her boot out of the window. She did it on the first throw. She was in the netball team, she would tell the interviewer. She had no idea if it had landed on the ground or stayed on the roof, but she didn't hear a thud. Not only that, if her boot landed on the drive or somewhere, they would know. 'Jessica Green was last seen wearing a blue coat and ankle-length black boots'. She shouted help about twenty times but gave up. It was as quiet as the grave.

She took the six-inch-long shard out from under the pillow. She almost wished Miles would come back; she was ready. She was so thirsty but didn't dare drink any of the water. Not even from the other bottle. She had to be awake when he opened the door. She wouldn't give him a chance to come in the room, and she went through it in her mind. Stab and shove, then run like the wind. It would sound so good on one of those true-life documentaries, she told herself. She had to be found and be alive to be famous. She'd settle for a cuddle with her mummy right now. Her mum and dad must be so upset. They will have phoned all my friends, and mum will be crying her eyes out. Work will have been interviewed by now. Saying how much she was valued as a worker.

She closed her eyes and wondered which photo Mum would have given the police to find her and to the press for the front pages. She just hoped it was the one taken on her twenty-first birthday, where she was smiling and had on her gorgeous black and white dress.

In a council house on the outskirts of Gorebridge, Mr Green asked his wife, "Have you heard from our Jessica?"

"Not a thing. She can be so selfish, not like Holly. She's always ringing to see how we are. I'm trying to think when was the last time we saw her. She's probably enjoying herself at the fayre today with all her mates."

"Must be a month ago. I'm not chasing after her; she'll ring when she wants something, I dare say."

On the other side of town one of her house-mates was remarking how Jessica had gone away and not done her washing up before she went. Typical, they all agreed. She wasn't even answering her phone. That's the trouble with Jessica; she never thinks of anyone but herself.

At Hope Bay Holidays, a supervisor was telling one of the girls that Jessica Green had had her last chance. She'd thrown a sickie once too often. He'd send her an email - she was fired.

Chapter 10

IT WAS A GOOD THING THAT THE GHOSTLY TRIO OF Abigail, Terry, and Suzie could walk through the front door of Jim's flat, as the other side was covered with a mound of letters, bills, and papers. No one had missed him yet, it would seem. Terry couldn't help but think that in his day it wouldn't have happened. An extra milk bottle outside and the neighbours, or the milkman himself would have been on the case. Supermarkets had a lot to answer for. They all went in slowly, for fear of seeing a dead Jim lying in a pool of blood. Nothing in the hall at least.

Once inside the flat, it was a lot smaller than they had expected and, to be honest, a lot more untidy. Jim was obviously not houseproud. All the furniture looked old, and the sofa's cushions and arms were well-worn. The television on the wall was the only thing that looked like it had cost a lot.

Abigail did not know Jim as well as the others, so asked, "Did Jim live alone? I take it he did looking at this. It's definitely lacking the woman's touch."

Terry knew a bit more. "He was divorced, and his wife still lives in their house. It's on the other side of Gorebridge, I think.

No kids that I know of. He's never said about visiting her, so maybe they were estranged. Looks like he got a raw deal, if this flat is anything to go by."

"You're not kidding. This looks like it was in happier days." Abigail pointed out a framed photograph on the wall of a girl and boy. It showed a young Jim and his older sister at a funfair. They looked very alike and were about nine or ten. Why hadn't his sister noticed he was missing? Maybe they were estranged as well. They would need to speak to her and the ex-wife as soon as they started his investigation in the near future. The photograph of them was the only thing that was personal, apart from a pile of unopened mail on the table. At least there was no body in the flat. A Breather would have been able to smell if there was, so Terry told them.

The bedroom was no tidier. The bed was strewn with clothes as if he had left in a hurry.

"Has he been robbed, or is it always like this?" said Abigail. "Don't forget he said he's paid mostly in cash, so there should be some money here somewhere or maybe that's what they were looking for. And keep an eye out for his phone and car keys." Abigail asked Suzie, as she was the only Mover, to have a good look around. It took all her energy, but she managed to search his drawers and cupboards. She even checked in the fridge and freezer. There wasn't a lot of food, and the only thing in the fridge was cans of beer. They all felt rather sorry for Jim. He was such a nice man, and all they had seen so far was how lonely he had been. At least he had a chance of happiness with Lillian.

"Look at this," said Terry. "Now being a man I can understand Jim and his housekeeping. When you live on your own, there's no one to tidy up for, or nag you to do it, so I'm just wondering why someone who probably couldn't cook an egg, would have a ceramic container for flour? Can you see him baking a cake or pancakes?"

"Bravo, Terry. We'll make a Jessica Fletcher of you yet."

Suzie managed to get the top off and tipped out a roll of notes. "You were right. Must be his savings, bless him. So we can rule out robbery."

"Unless the burglars weren't as good as us. We'd better leave it in there for the police, if they ever find out about him. I must remember to tell Hayley that Tom should drop some hints about Jim. He could have walked in on burglars, but we've got enough on our plate at the moment. I'll promise Jim that we will crack his murder when we've solved mine. If we ever do. But I feel we're getting closer. I've got this nagging feeling that I've seen something important already. I need to think, so let's get back to the library quick smart."

Parking was always a problem in Gorebridge town centre, but 'Hill & Stonehouse - Chartered Accountants' had its own car park around the back. Hayley introduced herself to the model-type receptionist. "Morning. Hayley Bennett. I've got an appointment with Mr Hill at ten o'clock."

"You can go straight up. It's the first door on the left. He's expecting you."

Nathan Hill was indeed a very handsome man, thought Hayley. But in a way it made him seem even more suspicious. He had the look of a man who had got everything in life that he wanted - looks, brains, and good luck more than likely. If he always got his own way in life, maybe that would be enough to hit back at someone that tried to stop him.

"Take a seat, Mrs Bennett. Can I get you a coffee or anything?"

"No, thank you. I'm fine."

"What can I do for you?" he said with a dazzling smile. Hayley almost forgot what she was supposed to be saying.

"I'd like to make a will. I've been left an inheritance by an old aunt and need to do something with it. It might as well be earning interest."

"How much are we talking about?"

"About fifty thousand," Hayley lied.

"Lucky you. Yes, that's far too much to just let it sit there." Hayley hardly listened as he went on to tell her about various stocks, shares and bonds. She remembered to nod from time to time.

"I'd need to discuss it with my husband."

"Will he be the main beneficiary of your will? If there's property and children involved, we would need to make another appointment."

"No children but we own our house. I want Tom to make his will out as well. I bumped into a friend of mine recently - Tania Ashwin. It was very sad. Her husband committed suicide and left her in an awful mess. All their money had gone. Have you heard of him? It was in the paper."

"Ashwin? No. I don't think I have. How awful." Hayley noticed he rubbed his nose, a sure sign of lying.

"He should have come to you," she said, smiling. "Not only that, I'm starting to feel a bit mortal myself these days, because another one of my friends passed away recently. She was my dressmaker - Abigail Summers."

"Oh dear. Sounds like you are unlucky to know, Mrs Bennett. Perhaps you shouldn't become one of my clients." There sounded a slight threat in his voice, Hayley thought. And he didn't admit to knowing Abigail. That was very odd if he was innocent. "Take these leaflets and have a think about it and then make an appointment to make a will, as well as moving the money. Perhaps your husband could come in at the same time. What does your husband do?"

"He's a gardener." Hayley wasn't a very good liar at the best of times and nearly rubbed her nose as well and wondered if she had turned red. She got up very abruptly and said, "Thank you so much, Mr Hill. You've given me a great deal to think about. I'll make an appointment sometime next week."

Nathan Hill smiled but didn't believe it for a second. Who the hell was she? After she had gone, he looked out of his window into the car park below and took a note of her car and number plate - a red mini, EP03 VYN. Just in case, he told himself.

Half an hour later, Monica was also wondering who the hell this woman was. Hayley had turned up at the door and brazenly walked past her.

"Sorry to turn up like this, but I just had to pay my last respects to somebody. Are you one of Abigail's relatives?"

"Monica, her niece. And who are you? I'm too upset to see anyone if you wouldn't mind going. We're both completely devastated."

Yeah right, thought Hayley. "Abigail was a dear friend and I was her medium. I did warn her that something was about to happen, but she didn't listen to me. If only she had," she lied.

Monica immediately looked interested and said she could sit down. "Did you really? I love anything to do with the supernatural. I'm a real believer. And don't get me started on UFOs. I'm sure I saw a flying saucer once. My husband said it was a balloon, of course. But balloons don't go along and then suddenly shoot up, do they? I'd love to have a reading one day, if it's not too expensive. Do you feel anything about me?"

"I sense the letter A is important to you. But that could mean Abigail."

Monica's eyes widened. "No! My husband's name is Aaron. Do you sense anyone in this room? Sometimes it goes freezing in here. I hope it's not Abigail's ghost. I hope she doesn't resent us moving in. She died upstairs, you know."

"She may still come at times. This was her home for all of

her life and she loved it here. I feel this vase is important to her."

"I told Aaron it wasn't me! Once it tipped right over on its own. I knew it was her. What is she trying to tell us?"

Hayley closed her eyes theatrically and held up her hands. "She's here now and wants to find out how she died. She's saying she was in bed and then she couldn't breathe and doesn't know why."

"Oh my God, she died of carbon monoxide poisoning. Tell her it was an accident. Even the police say it was. Nothing to do with us."

"What's that, Abigail? She says how do you know it wasn't your husband?... Is that so? She said someone took the detectors off the wall."

"Oh my God, we didn't even know that. And Aaron can be annoying and go on about things, but he's a coward and no way would he live in this house if he'd killed her. I'm the one that has to get rid of the spiders. Not only that, we were together practically all the time when it happened. And it was his dad's sister. He would take her house but not her life. Make sure Abigail believes me, please."

"She does. Don't worry, she believes you."

"Thank God for that. And tell her not to come again, please. I've got goosebumps just thinking about it."

"Sorry, I can't promise that. She feels she still has the right to be here. But I'll ask her not to."

"I would really appreciate that, thank you. Have you got anything else you can tell me?"

Monica was shocked to hear what she said. It came to Hayley through a vision of a nursery upstairs. "You are going to have a little girl in the new year." But the next thing she made up in the hope of it being true, "And you will call her Abigail."

.   .   .

Jim and Lillian arrived at the library just after Hayley. They were holding hands, and Betty said what they were all thinking, "Aww, young love." Suzie and Terry shared a happy look.

They both looked a bit embarrassed and let go but took a seat next to one another.

"You're just in time," began Abigail. "Hayley is just going to tell us what happened when she went to see Nathan Hill. What did you think of him, Hayley?"

"Gorgeous - obviously. But I did not like him at all. Definitely untrustworthy. I brought up Andrew Ashwin and you, Abigail, and he denied knowing either of you."

"How rude! Well, that's a point against him for sure," said Abigail. Terry smirked and thought he would like Nathan.

Betty added, "Now that is funny. Why would anyone deny knowing you? And we know he advised Andrew Ashwin. So he's hiding something."

Hayley blew out her cheeks. "Yes, he's slimy, a liar and shifty for sure, but I don't get a feeling of him being a murderer. He was very suspicious of me when I asked him about you. I wouldn't want to bump into him on a dark night."

"I would," said Betty, with a twinkle in her eye.

"Betty! Behave," laughed Hayley.

"I still think it's possible it's him, though. He's got a motive for both. If he killed Ashwin, or forced him to kill himself, you might have been the only one to know of the connection," said Jim.

"I agree," added Lillian and took his hand again. "With all their money and titles, the Hattons don't need to bump anyone off. Much more likely to be him, as Jim said."

Abigail looked at Jim and said, "I hope you don't mind, but we stopped by your flat earlier. Terry had an idea that your body might still be in the flat, but it wasn't. We didn't want you to be there in case it was. I know how much it hurts to go back to your old haunts, if you excuse the pun." Terry shook his head at another one of her jokes. "I'm so sorry, Jim. We will definitely find out what happened to you after my mess is all sorted," Abigail promised.

"I'm grateful you did go and look. For some reason I've got an awful feeling of dread every time I think about my flat. But don't worry. Let's focus on you for now." As usual, Terry thought and rolled his eyes.

Betty clapped her hands together. "So what are the clues?"

"We know someone got into my house in broad daylight," said Abigail. "Gwen, next door, saw a young bloke in a cap and overalls go up to my house. So that puts the men, and my nephew, Aaron in the frame. But when you think of it, that doesn't mean it wasn't a woman or anyone else behind it. He could have been hired by any of them to murder me."

"People will do anything for a wad of cash these days," said Jim. Lillian agreed as she'd seen the worst of what man could do to each other in the emergency room at the hospital.

"Look what someone did to you, Jim," said Betty. "A young workman, just trying to make his way in life."

Abigail looked thoughtful. "That is so true. Could they have been after your car, Jim? Maybe a car-jacking?"

"No. I've only got an old van. So that definitely wasn't the reason."

"We'll investigate it soon, Jim, I promise, won't we?" Betty said, looking round at them all.

"I'll have a word with Tom as well. He might have heard something, Jim. Sorry, Abi, where were we?"

Abigail closed her eyes and concentrated hard. "I'm still thinking of Nathan Hill. Did he panic when he heard that Andrew Ashwin had topped himself? Maybe, but why would he risk all the good things in life? He's made his money by being ruthless, so he wouldn't care what people think."

"Agreed," said Jim. "What about Aaron and Monica?"

"I think it's them," said Betty. "They'd lost their home, and they would know exactly where the flue and the gas detectors were. I bet they have a key too. And look how quick they got in there. You said yourself that they'd already started chucking all your stuff out within days of you dying. You know what they say, if it looks like a swan, walks like a swan, quacks like, okay you can have that one," she laughed. "But you haven't told us how you got on with Monica, Hayley. Did you go and see her?"

"Yes, I was getting to that. She tried to get rid of me until I said I was psychic. She was far too interested to be guilty. She didn't think Aaron could have done something like that and was sure it was an accident. But Aaron can't be ruled out yet. Oh, and by the way, hun, you're going to be an auntie."

"Really? How wonderful. Now I'm even more determined to find out who killed me. I would have been such a fun, cool aunt. I could have made them lots of dressing-up clothes and little cute toys."

"And it will be a little girl."

"Well, they better name her after me, that's all I can say," said Abigail sadly.

"They will. I have a feeling, hun."

Suzie asked Abigail, "I don't think it's Aaron because wouldn't your neighbour have recognised him as being the bloke at your house?"

"Good point. But out of her window, she might not have had the best view. I wanted it to be them, even if we are related. But not now they are having a baby. You can't choose your family as they say. And while we were there, they never talked like they had committed a murder, did they? Surely they would have shown more signs of fear. Watching the news or something. The only feelings I saw were happiness that they'd got my house and what they were going to do to it, so I don't think I'll forgive them yet. When this is over, remind me to go and haunt them, Suzie. There must be something I can do."

"I'll come with you; I'm an excellent Haunter." Suzie grinned.

"So if it's not them, we're down to the Hattons."

"Lord and Lady Muck were my next choice," said Betty.

"I'll tell you what we haven't talked about, it's that photo of Helen on the boat," said Terry. "If it was on the sea somewhere. Could this have to do with drugs or something?"

"I hadn't considered that at all, if I'm honest," said Abigail, thinking hard and fast. "Helen doesn't look much of a drug baron. Could be a motive maybe. As for opportunity, I know they've got an alibi. But that could be because they've gone to Scotland for just that reason and paid someone else to do the murder for them. They've got the means. God knows they can afford it. As a magistrate, he could have easily got the name of someone willing who had come up before him. No, it was definitely a gun for hire, as they say. Let me just think for a minute." Abigail leaned back and closed her eyes. She started moving her hands about as if she was playing chess.

Terry looked at the others and rolled his eyes. Lillian and Jim looked at each other and giggled.

"Are you alright, dear?"

"Yes, thank you, Betty. I think I've got it," she said excitedly. "Yes, it was definitely a hired killer. And I'm telling you now, I think, well, I know, exactly what happened!"

"Really?" Betty said. "Are you sure?"

"There's no way you could know that," snapped Terry.

"I had all these bits and pieces in my head, and I saw something today and then I heard something else, and suddenly it all fell into place. I didn't want to say anything at the time because I just needed to find something out."

Jim and Lillian looked at each other and raised their eyebrows. They had no idea what was going on. "Go on then. Tell us what you think happened."

"It's all to do with the fact that Lord Angus should never have inherited."

"Didn't I say that it was him?" said Lillian, triumphantly. Although none of them could actually remember it.

"Oh no, Lillian. Not Angus. It was The Honourable Charles."

Chapter 11

"ARE YOU SURE, ABIGAIL?" NONE OF THEM LOOKED particularly convinced or even impressed.

"Deadly."

"Was it the photo of the red-haired man? So that really was Charles' dad like Betty said?" asked Terry.

"Nope. Angus was definitely his father. And it was him, Angus, that shouldn't have inherited. And if he didn't, then Charles couldn't."

"Now you've totally lost me. Start at the beginning, Abigail."

"It was the old photo at the church, remember? It had Angus with his parents and his little brother. I had a feeling there was something we were missing at the time. But when we were in your flat, Jim, I saw a lovely photo of you and your sister."

"I know the one - at the fair when we were teenagers."

"That's the one. We assumed she was older than you because she was taller, but she could have been younger. But think back to the picture we saw at the Hall, Betty. There was the father with a babe in arms and a little red-haired toddler who was holding his mother's hand. We might not know who was older in your photo, Jim, but you can't confuse a baby for a toddler. And although Charles has the red-haired gene that runs in his family, his dad hasn't, so Angus must be the babe in arms. So if that's the case, and Graham is older, why did Angus inherit and not Graham?"

"I thought he had died young?" said Jim. "I remember someone saying that."

"He did. But what is young? I would say I've died young and you. I must admit I thought he was about ten or something. But Hayley found out he had a daughter named Caroline who went to Scotland for the twentieth-year anniversary of her parents' deaths, so he couldn't have been that young. And Angus told Hayley that he had become Lord Amerston years ago. Graham died, but I think he died just after his father, so the title had already been passed to him."

"But wouldn't Angus have inherited anyway as the only boy after his brother died?"

"No. Caroline would. It would be Graham and then his child - son or daughter. In Scotland, a female can inherit as long as there are no boy siblings, younger or older. And she was an only child. Aristocracy is still very misogynistic down here.

Caroline was young at the time so she wouldn't have a clue she was cheated out of her rightful future. Could be she's even younger than her cousin, Charles. And remember Hayley found out that her parents both died together. I'm not saying that Angus and Helen arranged the boat accident; they just saw the opportunity to have it all for themselves and their son. Even if Angus had run the estate until Caroline was eighteen, Charles would have been cut out. No money, no house, and no title. Look what they've done to Caroline; they haven't shared their good fortune with her. Although she might not have been so mean. They lived in the Highlands, so a backhander to a lawyer, and they could get away with it, no doubt. She could, in theory, have taken their family home for herself, and they'd be stuck in a cottage on the estate. She would even be the sole owner of Chiltern Hall."

"What makes you think Charles even knew? How would he find out?"

"I've just realised how. The photo! He saw that photo himself, probably years ago, and worked it out. He's at Cambridge, so he must have a good brain. But you don't have to be a rocket scientist. That's why I had to die in case I did the same. I can remember asking if that was him in the picture, and he said no, it was his uncle. But I never would have worked out who was who. I'm as thick as a plank compared to him. Which makes what he did even more ridiculous."

Terry shook his head. "But he was in Scotland. In fact, he stayed an extra day."

"I know he did. That's the clever thing. He had a reason for that. His parents could give him an alibi, but they didn't know that he actually came back to commit the other murder."

They all said, "What murder?" Everyone was frowning and looking at each other.

Terry jumped in. "Oh, you mean Andrew Ashwin. But what did he have to do with the Hattons?"

"No, not Andrew, Terry. He had to get rid of the man he paid to kill me. He didn't want to pay the rest of the money he owed or to live with the threat of being blackmailed by him?"

"But who are you talking about? We're never going to find him. It literally could be anyone."

"I know exactly who he is. I'm sorry to tell you; it's Jim!"

They all started talking at once. Lillian looking annoyed, Suzie upset, and the others apologising to Jim.

"I can't believe you would even think I'm capable of killing anyone, let alone you. I've never hurt anyone in my life," said Jim with a bewildered look on his face.

"I can hardly believe it myself, and I honestly think you have no memory of it. But just hear me out, all of you, please. I missed all the early clues, and if I hadn't gone to your flat, I probably would never have known."

"Me and Terry were with you, and we didn't see a thing," Suzie snapped.

"I thought I'd seen something, but I couldn't think what until Jim said 'People will do anything for a wad of cash'. Well, I worked for myself and took cash, and I'd shove it in a tin when I was paid, and it built up and up. Notes and coins. Not a neat little bundle of cash like the one we found in his flat."

"Maybe he counted it and rolled it up ready for the bank," said Lillian, protecting Jim.

"This was a perfect roll, and all the notes were twenties. Like a payout for work done. I would estimate it looked like at least a thousand." Jim was looking down and shaking his head. Abigail carried on, "When Betty called you a workman, it made me think of when Gwen said she saw a man in overalls. Well, you're wearing those khaki jeans with the pockets down the legs. I think Gwen would think they're overalls, however much they cost. That's why I asked about your car. That was the final clue. She also said she'd seen a white van in the road. I know you can't remember, but please try, Jim. I'm really hoping I'm wrong. What's the last thing, or more to the point, what's the first thing you remember when you came to?"

"You are wrong. I've never met Charles. But I'll try. I was... I know I was at the Greyhound pub. I was meeting someone. Who was it? I don't know. I don't know."

"I'm sorry, Jim. I think it was Charles. You and him had met at the Hall when you did some work last year. Or at least he saw you there. He likes his beer too. Hayley said he spent all day in the beer tent at the fayre, and your fridge is full of it. Stands to reason you would bump into him at the pub. The Greyhound is not that far from the Hall. So Charles could easily have arranged to meet you there, or conveniently bump into you, to put the idea to you and give you the first payment. And you went back there that night, after you'd done it, to get the rest of the money."

"For God's sake, I would never... never..." Realisation slowly showed in his eyes. It was coming back to him. "I didn't. Oh my God." His shoulders slumped, and he started to sob.

"Tell us what happened, Jim. You're amongst friends now."

"I was drinking one night in the pub. On my own as usual lately. I knew him from the Hall when I was there and had seen him at different bars, enough to pass the time of day. He offered me the chance to make some money. A lot. Then enough to disappear for a while. Go to Spain or somewhere. I had a feeling it wasn't a building job. But I was sick of working hard for a pittance and living in a poky flat. Why shouldn't I? He said block the flue and take the batteries out. He'd seen there were two detectors when he went round there. And it wasn't going to kill her, he said. Just make her a bit ill to pay her back for dumping him, then he'd go round and save her. Charles said he was madly in love with her and she'd cheated on him. I'd been there, I told him. I believed him and didn't want to face the truth, not forgetting the money was more than I'd earned in months, so I said okay. He gave me the first thousand and told me the name and address. He didn't write it down so they couldn't trace it back to him."

"How could you?" shouted Lillian.

"I don't know. I seem different now. I had money troubles, so I must have felt like it was my way out. Do I have to say anymore?"

"Definitely," said Abigail tersely. "I want to know it all."

"You probably know it already. I waited for you to leave and went round the back and blocked up the outside flue and then got through the kitchen window."

"How? I never leave windows open. Even when I'm home I'm always manic about safety."

"In a house of that age, those old wooden frames are easy. If you bang hard enough, the latch jumps off. So I climbed in and took both detectors off. He'd told me to take the batteries out, but it would take too long. I'd seen the neighbour looking at me out of her window as I arrived, so I just wanted to get out fast. Then I turned the pressure up full. I knew if not, it could take days or weeks for you to even notice. I needed that money. He'd promised to keep an eye on you and look out for signs of headaches and that. I thought Charles could put them back after he had saved you, in a day or two. I saw an extractor fan in there, so I cut the electric off to that as well, in case you used it."

"I lived for three more nights, Jim. A slow horrible death."

"I'm so ashamed, Abigail. I met him that night to get the rest of my money at ten, in the Greyhound's car park. I should have known I couldn't trust him. He pulled in and said my money was in the boot. It was quite dark, but I could just make out a big holdall in there so I grabbed it, but I could feel it was empty. Then I felt a pain like never before, and he pushed me in. I remember wondering why it had stopped hurting if I'd been stabbed. He drove for a while and got out."

"This is good, Jim. You might know where your body can be found," urged Betty.

"I know where it is now. Charles dragged me out and threw me down this shaft, like an old well. It had a board over it."

"But where was it, do you know?"

Jim nodded. "I did work near there. It's by their old stable block on the estate. They don't keep horses anymore, so I would never have been found."

"What we couldn't work out was why nobody knew you were missing? What about your sister?"

"I haven't seen her for months. What is it they say? Never a borrower nor a lender be. She'd bailed me out many a time, but even she'd had enough. If not her, then her eighteen-stone husband. I owed her money, and she didn't want to lend me any more, so I couldn't even see her for a drink or anything after that. I'd got myself in a bit of a state. It had gotten that bad I couldn't even open any mail. The thought that it might be another bill would send me into a cold sweat. I had to get away, and Charles offered me a chance."

Betty smiled sadly. "You were desperate, and that pig took advantage of you. Who knows what any of us would do with our backs against the wall."

"That's kind of you, but I don't deserve it. I'm sorry, Lillian. I didn't want to hurt you, I hope you know that. You'll never know how sorry I am. But you'll get justice, Abigail; he threw the knife and my phone down the well after me. It's the last thing I saw before it went dark. He wasn't wearing gloves, you see."

Abigail put her hands across her chest, "Yes, we've got him."

By now, Jim was inconsolable, but no one went to comfort him. He turned his head. He could no longer look at his friends. He locked eyes with Lillian, but she walked away. The thought they'd been in the company of a murderer had shocked them to the core.

Terry was the first to see what happened next. A grey swirl in the shape of a tunnel had appeared. It sounded like a howling wind. Jim got to his feet with a terrified look on his face. "I'm so sorry. I'm so sorry," and backed into it, as if it was pulling him in, and he disappeared from sight."

"What happened, Terry? I never wanted that."

"That, Abigail, was, as they say, a hell of your own making. When his spirit realised what his soul had done, he was done for. The guilt gets them every time. He'll not be back. I've seen it before."

Lillian's eyes flashed at Abigail. "Everything was fine till you came. Why don't you just go back to where you came from?"

"I wish I could, Lillian, but that's not going to happen thanks to Jim, is it?"

Abigail felt the chill in the air even more than usual. They seemed to blame her more than Jim or even Charles. She stood up and walked out. She would have loved to slam the door behind her, but she couldn't even do that now.

Abigail took to the streets. She'd show them. She might not even bother going back. There must be somewhere else in the whole of Becklesfield that she could go. Maybe she could hang out at the pub. That was the hub of the village anyway. Much more interesting than a library. That or the Post Office. If you wanted to know something, chances are Miss Spindle would be the first to know.

And didn't they think she would care that it was amiable Jim? She could hardly believe it herself, but she knew she was right. She'd always had a logical mind and had solved crosswords from a young age. Her brother said she should play chess, but she never fancied that. Too time-consuming for a start. That was what she liked about the dressmaking; it was like a puzzle. Taking a piece of material and turning it into something beautiful. She would never do those things again. Perhaps she should move on. The others were all annoyed with her. They definitely had shot the messenger, she realised. And she was getting rather fond of Terry. Although, they were in shock. Why was she feeling so guilty? It was because Jim had become a friend already and could have been something even more for Lillian. So much for her judgement.

She turned left by the church and saw Hayley's house. Abigail wondered if she had got back home yet. She would understand and was so easy to talk to. Anyway, she wanted to hear that she was right. Hayley had worked the hardest out of all of them to get the answers. Tom's car was not there so she went in calling out as she did. She needed a sympathetic ear, not the accusing looks she'd had at the library.

Hayley had been home about ten minutes and had been really shocked to hear about Charles and was surprised, as the others were, that Jim had turned out to be a murderer. Unlike the others, she didn't seem to blame Abigail and gave her a big pretend hug when she saw her.

"Come on, hun, let's go and sit in the conservatory. What a kerfuffle that all was. I feel exhausted from the drama."

"Tell me about it. Jessica Fletcher never got this much aggro."

"It had to come out. I never met Charles, so I didn't get a reading on him. He spent the day of the fayre in the beer tent with his friends, and I was hoping to talk to him, but what with that boy going missing and Tom turning up, it totally went out of my head. Same as with Jim, I didn't know him as well as the others. Did you suspect Charles from the start?" asked Hayley.

"Not at all. To be honest, not until I suspected Jim after I saw all that money. Then the puzzle kind of made sense. They had met before, and once I'd seen the photo at Jim's of him and his sister, it all clicked into place. Looking at where he lived, I could see he was in debt and unhappy. So I had a feeling that something was all wrong. It didn't match up to the Jim I thought he was. I had to find out one thing before I said it out loud, and that was to ask Jim if he had a car, and when he said no, he only had a van, I definitely knew it was him.

At the fitting, I thought how nice and chatty Charles was. Not at all snobbish. But was he keeping me talking to take my mind off what I'd seen in that photo? He gave me more credit than I deserve. I'm not that clever."

"But you did work it out, Abi."

"In the end and not on my own. But I did like a gossip when I was pinning, so you never know. Maybe I did ask him about his family and the photograph. Or did I say something about Lords and Ladies? I really can't remember. And it hadn't occurred to me that he could have got the idea when he came to pick up their sewing. I left him on his own downstairs when I went up to get it. Did he notice the boiler and alarm then and come up with the idea? What an idiot he is. If he hadn't killed Jim, he might never have been caught. He was hoping to put the detectors back the next day, after the supposed joke. Charles had told him to take the batteries out and not take the whole thing, but he was worried he had been seen so he did what was quickest. I wouldn't have been suspicious then either. I reckon they will find them in Jim's van, and that will connect the two murders. That will really prove who did it. He'll spend the rest of his life in prison. If an expensive lawyer doesn't get him off."

"I really don't get the sense that his parents knew anything about it. I did feel Helen had troubled waters ahead at her reading, but I chose to tell her she was going on a long boat trip."

"I don't think they had a clue," agreed Abigail. "I'm sure they would have done anything to protect their son, but wouldn't have condoned murder. Helen did hint that he was headstrong and did as he pleased."

"I suppose Caroline will inherit now?"

"For sure. Hopefully she will let her aunt and uncle stay in one of the houses, and I expect Angus will be done for fraud. I think after Charles' trial they will move back to Amerston Manor in Scotland. Do you think there's enough for DCI Johnson to open both cases?"

"I'm sure of it. He'll want to get all the glory. There will be the fingerprints and DNA on the bag and knife. I'll get Tom to find out. I rang him as soon as I got home. I told him your ideas and he's got to think of a way to pass it on. He took a bit of persuading."

"Jim's mobile, with any texts between them, is in the well with him."

"And now they have Jim's fingerprints too, they can check against any at your house. Maybe on the boiler and the window."

"He died instantly when he was stabbed, and the heart would have stopped pumping out blood, but there will be enough in his boot for the forensic people to find, I'm sure. Lillian's really annoyed with me, I'm not sure I can go back there. They were really serious apparently."

"I could feel a bit of chemistry between Jim and Lillian."

"I had no idea until Suzie said about it at the fayre. But I feel no animosity towards him. Is that wrong? But I couldn't let him get off, could I? Justice has to be done. Charles might even give a full confession, and then Lillian might forgive me. He will be absolutely gobsmacked that someone worked it all out. Let alone how someone knew where the body was."

"Tom might say he had an anonymous phone call from a poacher that saw someone dragging a body out of a car at the Hall. DCI Johnson is going to be so mad that Tom was involved again. He's already caught the eye of the Chief Constable for finding the missing little boy. The boss likes nothing better than good press. He's told Tom to sit his sergeant's exam."

"You don't have to be psychic to see a good future ahead for him, Hayley."

"I wish I could offer you a cup of tea, hun. You must need one."

"A wine would be better," Abigail said, wistfully. "But I'd better go. I've got some decisions to make. As the song says, shall I stay or shall I go now? I don't know if I'll be welcome at the library anymore so maybe I should cross. And I don't want to be here when Tom gets back. I get the feeling he doesn't like me much either. I thought I'd be a bit more popular over on this side, to be honest."

"You're marvellous, hun. You've done so well to work it out. Charles would have got away with it, and I've got a feeling that Caroline might have been next on his list, because one day she may have realised that the dates don't match up. Who knows what Little Lord Fauntleroy would have got up to in the future. I don't know a lot about a psychopathic mind, but I do know if they can get away with it once, they will carry on."

"We all did well. Especially you. Did they ever find Andrew's suicide note?"

"Yes, I'm pleased to say. Exactly where I said, on the fridge. He's moved on now. I'm sure his family will too."

"That is good to know. Now you will tell us when you have any news from Tom, won't you? You know where to find us. I better go."

"I'm not looking forward to explaining all this to Tom. I hope he believes it and can think of how to pass it on without getting in a pickle. He's going to have to tell a lot of little white lies. But it's all for a good cause. Go on, Abi, you get off and please cheer up," Hayley said kindly. "My sixth sense tells me that when they've thought it through, you'll be back in their good books."

"I don't even feel like making a joke about libraries, so I must be depressed. Bye, Hayley, and thanks for listening to a sad old spirit."

"Bye, hun. I'll see you soon."

Abigail decided to have a slow walk around the beautiful village where she had lived all her life, just in case she decided to leave. She stopped outside the Becklesfield Primary School where she had been so happy. When she was a pupil, there were only ten to a class; now they had built a new extension to the old building. In the playground, someone had drawn a game of hopscotch with chalk. She was surprised the kids of today would still want to play that.

The next memory lane she went down was the one to the village green. Here were the oldest houses that were made of stone. Some of them had thatched roofs and lattice windows and were worth a fortune, even though the rooms were tiny and they took an awful lot of upkeep. It was getting late and not many people were about. She went over to the stocks where the locals were once put for misdemeanours. How she'd like to put Charles in there. She wouldn't be throwing tomatoes, that was for sure. The moonlight shone on the pond, the centrepiece of the green, and she felt sad that she wouldn't enjoy the beauty of life in the same way again. Yes, she could see it all but she'd no longer enjoy the sunshine or sit outside the pub with a glass of wine or smell the flowers. Oh, shut up, she told herself. When had she ever smelt the flowers? Stop feeling sorry for yourself. It is what it is.

Her next stop was the swings on the edge of the park. The see-saw and monkey bars had gone and were replaced by a roundabout and wooden climbing frame with ropes attached. Far safer probably, Abigail thought. And where had the concrete gone? Now there was soft rubber, she noticed. She couldn't ever remember children breaking bones or cutting their heads open all the time. Maybe they used to be made of sterner stuff. The swings were the same, so she sat on the one in the middle to have a think about life and, most importantly, death. An old lady with a dog walked a bit faster when she saw it going backwards and forwards on its own. Abigail herself was no longer in a hurry. She didn't have to sit there sewing all hours of the day and night. There was always someone who wanted their work done quickly, if not the same day. She used to have a recurring nightmare where there would be someone knocking at the door for their wedding dress or outfit, and she hadn't started it yet. Or it would be literally covered in pins. That had actually happened once. She had started writing all her jobs down and ticked them off as she did them, but she still had nightmares. Maybe she was having one now - she was dead, and nobody liked her.

She felt something gently rubbing her legs, which felt good because she hadn't felt anything for a long time. It was a little cat, as ginger as they come. Was it a ghost or a real one? One could never be sure. She could pick it up, so it was a ghost like her.

"Hello, sweetie. What's your name? Have you got a collar? No. I think I'll call you Carrot. Do you want to come with me?" But it jumped off her lap and ran away, but then turned back and ran away again. "Is this like in those films? You want me to follow you?" A purr answered her. "Okay, wait for me then."

Abigail wasn't altogether sure she wanted to see what she was being led to. It could easily be the owner who had been dead for days, leaving poor Carrot to starve to death before she managed to escape. She slowed down when she thought she might be faced with a decayed and decomposing body. But Carrot wanted her to go with her, so she didn't have a choice. She seemed to be going towards the church that was locked up this time of night. Surely it wasn't Reverend Pete Stevens at the rectory. She racked her brains to remember if he or Mary had a cat. She didn't think so. But the cat passed through the stone wall and into the churchyard, which didn't do anything to quell Abigail's worries. In fact, things looked a lot worse as Carrot scampered to the far corner and stopped behind one of the gravestones - Emily May Paxton - she could just about make out in the dusk. Abigail dropped to her knees and saw a small, dark mass in the flattened long grass. She reached out tentatively and felt a small furry bundle that was cold and lifeless.

"I'm so sorry, Carrot, we're too late. Your baby's gone." The mother let out a slight purr and rubbed her nose over the kitten; then Abigail saw a tiny movement and, to her surprise, she heard a quiet meow. "It's alright, Carrot, it's alive, but I've got to get help." She leapt to her feet. "You stay here and I'll be back in two shakes of a kitten's tail."

Tom had been home about ten minutes and was enjoying his first cup of tea since breakfast, while Haylcy sat opposite him at the kitchen table. He was about to tell her how he'd told Sergeant Mills about Charles and Jim and that he had passed the information to Johnson, when he felt a blast of cold air. His news would have to wait… again. Tom let out a big sigh when he heard Hayley shriek, "You're kidding. I'll come now," then she rushed out the door, returning ten minutes later with a kitten wrapped in her cardigan. Apparently, they were keeping it and calling it Luna. He shook his head and thought most wives bring home doughnuts or maybe a takeaway, but no, not his wife. Although Hayley was always in those long floaty skirts, he couldn't help but feel that she actually wore the trousers!

Terry had to get out of the library as well; it had become a very sad place all of a sudden. It wasn't Abigail's fault; he knew that, and so did they really. They were all hurting, especially Lillian. She had met a lot of people since she'd arrived, but he'd never seen her take an interest in anyone like she did Jim. All she had cared about was Suzie. He knew she'd get over it if only for the little one's sake. Then hopefully, she would forgive Abigail.

It was then that he saw a new Dead. He was walking backwards and forwards in front of the shops. Just what he needed to take his mind off Jim.

"Can I help? Terry's the name."

"I really hope so. I don't know what happened. I think I was in a car accident." Terry took in the red face and the cuts over his eyes. That would have been his guess too.

"You know you're dead, right?"

"I saw my body, so yes," he replied irritably. "Somehow I knew I'd had it, but actually I think I'll go back there. I might just be in a coma. Do you think that's possible?"

"Anything is possible. What's your name, son?"

"Jason Masters. I just have this feeling that something is not right. Like I've left something turned on or there's something I had to do. It's no good. I'm going back. I shouldn't even be here. There must have been something wrong with the brakes. Someone's going to pay, you can be sure of that."

Terry shook his head as the man hurried back up the road. A lot were like that, especially his kind. The rich ones. They always thought they had more right to live as they could do whatever they wanted in life, and their lives were worth more. And he was definitely wealthy. You could tell that by his designer suit and shiny brown shoes. And even Terry knew that fancy gold watch of his was a Rolex.

"Look who needs a new home, Suzie?"

"Is he for me?" she said excitedly.

"She sure is. I only know it's a she because she had a little kitten before she died. I've never been a cat person, but this one is so cute. She's clever too; she showed me where her baby was and Hayley took him or her home. She's going to keep it, I think. It's a beautiful tortoiseshell one, not like its mummy. I've called this one Carrot but feel free to think of another name."

"I've never liked carrots, so definitely not that. He's got markings like a tiger, so I think Tiggy."

"That's perfect, far better than Carrot. Hayley's already called the kitten Luna. How would you like to come with me and Tiggy and meet him? He's so cute."

"What do you think, Lillian? Isn't he beautiful? I love him already. Thank you, Abigail."

"Lovely," said Lillian, through gritted teeth. She's trying to get around us now. If she comes between me and Suzie, she might be murdered again. I'll never forgive her for what she did to Jim. Lillian still didn't believe it. There will be other fingerprints on the knife. If it isn't a Hatton, it won't be Jim. Nothing could make her think that the sweet man who took her round the gardens of Chiltern Hall and told her he loved her was a heartless killer. She'd pay Abigail back if it took forever.

Chapter 12

Two days later, the librarian thought, "Oh no, it's that weird woman again, and now she's waving a newspaper!"

Hayley headed straight for the crime section, and Suzie ran around gathering everybody to the comfy chairs. She was glad to see that Abigail looked a little bit happier, and the others seemed to have forgiven her.

"How is little Luna?" asked Suzie. "Is Tiggy looking after her?"

"Yes, they're both fine. I took the kitten to the vet yesterday and found out Luna is actually a boy. And he's doing really well, thank goodness. It was a close thing."

"Every witch should have a cat," said Betty. "Oh, I'm sorry, I shouldn't have said that."

"Don't worry, I've been called far worse, and you're right. A few hundred years ago, I would have been dipped in the village pond for sure. I have a feeling that in a past life, I actually was, and Luna will make a very good familiar. Well, Tom has had a busy few days after he said he'd had a call from an anonymous poacher who saw someone throw what looked like a body down a well. Johnson was wild when the information came from him; I can tell you. Have you seen the Chiltern Weekly yet?" After admitting they hadn't, they begged her to read it aloud.

"BODY FOUND IN WELL AT STATELY HOME

After an anonymous tip-off, the body of builder, Jim Tate, was found in a well in the grounds of Chiltern Hall. He had been stabbed. Tate, aged 28, had not been seen since April 23rd. A man is helping police with their inquiries. He is thought to be a resident of Chiltern Hall. DCI Johnson will give a press conference when he has more information.
And there's a picture of Jim and the Hall."

"Great news," said Betty.

"His body needed to be found," said Suzie. "I would have hated to be in that well."

"Please thank Tom for us, Hayley. I don't know what we'd do without you two," said Abigail, sincerely.

"You're welcome, hun. But now I want to do something else for you all. Please let me help you pass over. Suzie, take my hand, and I can say a prayer, and hopefully, you can cross."

"I don't want to. Not yet. I'm waiting for my mum and brother to join me. I still visit, and I can tell mum likes it. She tells Jordan she can feel me holding her hand."

Lillian added, "Me neither. I met Suzie in the hospital that day and promised her I would always take care of her."

"And I need to tell the Deads they're dead, or all hell would break out," Terry said laughingly. "When I died all those years ago, I didn't know what had happened. I walked around for days not even knowing I was dead. I'd been brought up in an orphanage so I had no parents or grandparents to come for me. It took a man in the churchyard to explain to me what had happened. He's moved on since, but I still visit his grave. What about you, Betty?"

"Not on your nelly! I spent sixty years waiting hand and foot on my John, God rest his soul, and I died the week after him. I want some me-time. And I've had a ball the last two weeks. That just leaves you, Abigail."

"If you had asked me yesterday, I would have said yes, but now after seeing what we have all accomplished written in the paper, I think I'll stay. I know I have annoyed you all, but if you are willing, I have a great idea after hearing what Hayley read out. We're just getting started, and we could do an awful lot of good for people. We have a real knack for investigating, I reckon, and we make great detectives. And if I'm not mistaken, here is our first client."

They all turned to see a burly, young man barge through the wall. The reason Abigail thought he might be glad of their help was the fact that he had a large and bloody machete through his right shoulder.

"Sit down, please. This is Hayley, Terry, Suzie, Lillian, Betty, and I'm Abigail. Welcome to The Abi…I mean The… All Dead Detective Agency!"

"My name's Duncan," he said in a gruff voice. "Yeah, you can help me. Find the bastard that did this to me. I'm going to kill him."

"It's not exactly how we work, Duncan. It's more to give you peace of mind."

"I don't give a damn about that. I want to give him a piece of my mind and get the bastard." Oh dear, thought Abigail. This was not how she had imagined it. She feared her new detective agency might not be as easy as she had thought to run.

Hayley turned a page of the newspaper that she still held. "Hang on, Duncan, you're in luck." Well, not much, she thought after she had said it. "I read this earlier. We can help. Listen to this. 'A 22-year-old man was arrested last night charged with the murder of Duncan Sanders, 29 of Gorebridge. He is thought to be Matthew McKinley also of Gorebridge. He is being held at Gorebridge Central Police Station to help police with their enquiries."

"Cheers for that."

"Where are you going?" shouted Hayley after him.

"Where do you think? Gorebridge Central Police Station, to pay a special visit to my old friend, Matthew McKinley!"

"Another satisfied customer. I knew we'd be able to do it," lied Abigail. "But what do you all think? Our own detective agency. Are you all in?" Betty, Terry, and Suzie agreed straight away. "Lillian, I'd love it if you would be part of it. You know so much more than us about the medical stuff; we really need you."

"I don't suppose I have any choice if it's what the others want."

"Well, not exactly enthusiastic, but I'll take it. Hayley, we'll need your help as well. Please, please say yes."

"As long as we're doing good, you can count me in. I don't want to involve Tom every time though. He'd go mad."

"Of course not," said Abigail, somewhat untruthfully. "So we're all agreed we're calling it The Ab...I mean The All Dead Detective Agency, or the ADDA for short."

"That's a palindrome," said Suzie proudly.

"Well, we can't always agree on everything, dear," said Betty. That tickled them all, and Betty never minded.

But Terry had a point to make. "But we're not all dead, are we? There's Hayley and Tom to think of. I'm surprised you didn't call it The Abigail Summers Detective Agency."

"It never crossed my mind, Terry," said Abigail guiltily. "Unless you insist. You know me - others not self." Even she had to smile at that one. But was a little hurt when they all burst out laughing.

"What about The Deadly Detective Agency?" suggested Hayley.

"That's far better and much more catchy," said Terry, and they all agreed.

"Actually, I really need your help with something for a change," said Hayley. They all said they would love to be there for her. "I had an email through my website from someone right here in Becklesfield. Bear in mind that I don't tell my clients online where I live - too many trolls these days, and Tom would go mad if they just turned up for a reading. But the clients message me from all over, even America, so I took a special interest in this one as she's literally from here. I mean, what are the chances of that? Now this lady, Janette, sounded desperate and was asking for my help as she is being haunted by more than one ghost and can't sleep at night anymore. Apparently, it's relentless. She has to sleep with the lights on and her head under the covers."

"Poor love," said Betty.

"Yes, I feel for her. I've had my share of sleepless nights. I got the impression she is an older lady and she felt she was being threatened by them and had even seen things move on their own and noticed some strange smells. That's very common; it could be perfume or something like that. I can smell yours, Betty. What she wanted me to do was an exorcism. But I don't do those as such. I can say some prayers and light sage and mugwort or even give her reiki. As it's such a small village, I wondered if any of you had heard of a woman being tormented in that way? Especially you, Terry. You know most of the Deads around here."

Terry had a long think. "No, I can't say I do. What was her name again?"

"Janette. I thought if I got her address, would you go round there one night and catch him or her in the act, so to speak? And ask them to stop or move on, or at least find out the reason for it."

Abigail was more than happy to go. "It will be our first stake-out. I know we're supposed to take doughnuts and pee in a bottle, but it will be close enough. Find out her address, and we'll go round there. Does she live on her own?"

"She didn't say. I'll find out when I email her later."

"Well done, Hayley. We've got our next commission. Now we need to advertise if we're going to be successful. Do you think you could make us a sign and some posters, Suzie?"

"I could try. What do you want me to say on it?" she asked.

Abigail waved her hand expansively. "Nothing too compli-cated. In big letters, THE DEADLY DETECTIVE AGENCY, and then we'll need some sort of slogan like - 'We have the skills if you've been killed'. Then the library address at the bottom."

Terry shook his head. "It's not just murders that they need help with though, is it? It might be a missing will or a lost cat. Even finding a suicide note like Hayley found for Andrew Ashwin's family. Or hauntings to stop, or do."

Everyone fell silent to think of the best slogan themselves. Betty was the first one to come up with a good one.

"As you know, I've not long had my funeral, and the hymn my darling grandchildren chose for me was their favourite, All Things Bright and Beautiful.' Well, instead of 'All creatures great and small,' why not have 'All Problems Great and Small.'"

"That's so good, Betty. Don't let anyone tell you you're not good with words. That's marvellous. We've got all this paper here and none to make a poster with."

Once again Hayley could help; she went with Suzie to the newsagents for some paper and felt tips.

"I might have a new case for us as well," said Terry. "Not a whodunnit, I'm afraid. More of a 'whathashe forgotten.'"

"Sounds even more intriguing," said Lillian. "To be honest, I've had enough of murder for a while. I could do with a puzzle and hopefully a happy ending for someone."

"Do tell," urged Betty.

"The other day I met a chap who I think had been killed in a car accident. A rich guy, I might add, but I won't hold that against him. Not much anyway."

"All problems great and small, Terry. Perhaps we should add rich and poor," joked Abigail. "Carry on. What was his name?"

"Er, I think it was Jason Masters. He was all confused, naturally enough. But he had a feeling that something else was hanging over him. Like he'd left the gas on or something."

"There could be another passenger in the car maybe, who's just injured and no one has found him or her. It wouldn't be the first time."

"I don't know because he said he'd seen his body, and surely he would have noticed if someone else was there. He didn't actually ask for any help, so we'd better just leave it, Abigail."

"Agreed. We can only help those that ask. Although I am nosy and would love to know what happened. But you're right. We should keep well away."

Hayley came back through the door. Abigail looked up to see that the librarian had stopped her for a chat. "What did she want?"

"She said was I alright and would I be better off finding somewhere else to go in the daytime, where the care would be better, like a day centre?" They all burst out laughing. Definitely beyond help, the librarian thought. Now she's laughing at her own jokes.

"I'm going to start pretending I'm on my phone before I get carted away for talking to myself. But that doesn't work in here because we're not allowed to use them. At the May Day Fayre, I got some funny looks. It's my fault, I should at least pretend to be looking for a book." She went to the nearest shelf and grabbed a book. They all laughed at the title - 'The Invisible Man' by H.G. Wells.

"Come on, Suzie, if you make a few posters I'll help you put them up around town," said Hayley. Abigail was to find out that only Deads could see Suzie's writing. Good job too, they didn't want all the Breathers turning up! They had a feeling they were going to be busy enough.

There was more than one person in Becklesfield that afternoon that saw a long-haired, hippy-looking lady talking to herself and carefully sticking up posters on lampposts. More than likely her cat had gone missing, poor thing. So they thought they would take a look, to keep an eye open in case they saw it. But the paper was blank! Not a single thing on it. Bless her, so sad.

Chapter 13

THE NEXT DAY STARTED LIKE ANY OTHER, BUT THIS time Suzie and Lillian had gone to visit Suzie's mother and her brother, Jordan. Lillian still felt that she didn't want to be around Abigail too much. They took Tiggy with them as she had started to leave Luna a bit more lately. Betty thought she might run off and get lost going out of Becklesfield, but she needn't have worried, Tiggy walked by Suzie's feet and never left her side. So close that she even tripped her up a couple of times. It was a nice peaceful walk to where they lived in Little Chortle. They could have walked down the narrow, winding lanes but preferred to go across the meadows and share the fields with the sheep and their newborn lambs.

Suzie's family lived in a newly built estate on the edge of the pretty village. Sonia was a social worker, working with under-privileged children in Gorebridge. Since the loss of her own daughter, she felt she was more than qualified to help them and their parents. She knew herself how hard life could be. Her own husband and Jordan and Suzie's dad had left her when they were young. He had a new family now, but she didn't wish him any animosity. He had really taken the news of Suzie's death hard, and he knew he would never be able to get the time back that he had lost with her. Jordan too had gone off the rails for a while when his little sister had been run down by a drunk driver, but he had got back on track and was now studying hard at school and would be taking his exams next year. Even talk of him going to university.

It was Sonia's day off today, and as Jordan was at school, she thought to hell with the housework, she'd sit and watch some daytime TV. It was a nice summer's day, and she had all the windows open, but she felt a sudden chill in the air. She put her hand out in front of her and felt for what she knew would be there - a column of cold air. Suzie had come.

Back in the library, Abigail, Terry and Betty sat in their usual corner, feeling slightly bored. They had expected, or at least hoped that there would be a queue for the services of the newly-formed detective agency.

Abigail closed her eyes thoughtfully. "Maybe we should help your rich man, Terry. It will be something to do, if nothing else."

"How did you even know he was rich?" Betty sat forward and asked.

"He had a very nice Rolex. Even I know how much they are. Not that it worked anymore, of course. It stopped the second he died. And he was immaculately dressed in a suit and fancy brogues. It's nothing important, I dare say, just a bit of a mystery. He had blood coming from a head wound, and his face was bright red and starting to bruise. I've seen injuries like that, so I knew he'd been in a car accident. The fact he was starting to bruise told me he didn't die straight away. I learned that off Lillian. As I said, he was thinking he'd forgotten something important, or had to do something."

"Most of them think that, to be fair."

"I know. But there was something about him that felt different. I thought it might be that there was someone else in the car, but he would have seen that, as we said before."

"Terry was clever enough to get his name, so I think we should go and tell our very own angel, Hayley. She'll know what to do, and she's only round the corner. She's giving a talk about the paranormal to the Women's Institute at the church hall at two o'clock."

"Wonderful. I found all that stuff so interesting when I was alive. I watched all the ghost shows. I would love to see her in action," said an excited Betty.

"We'll stand at the back though. Hide behind a pillar or something. She might spot our orbs. Did you see what I did there? Spot our orbs?" Terry just groaned. Honestly, her jokes are atrocious!

The Becklesfield Church Hall was a new building next to the old church. New compared to the church, but still sixty years since it had been opened by the Mayor. Betty remarked she'd had her fortieth wedding anniversary party there. Abigail had started one of their line-dancing classes on a Thursday morning but found out she was hopeless, so gave that up. She was even worse at the tap dancing on a Friday afternoon. She was pleased to think she didn't have to worry about putting any weight on now or keeping fit.

There was a good turnout for 'The Psychic World of Hayley Moon'. Four rows of mostly women sat enthralled at her talk. She was explaining about the different angels and their names with the help of a slide show. Next, she went on to explain what the different colours of orbs meant. I must ask her what colour I am, thought Abigail. Hopefully not grey. I've always been particularly fond of pink. Not a bright one, a nice pastel would be perfect. Hayley seemed to be already surrounded with orbs and the classic mist of Deads. Poor Hayley. They all seemed to be vying for her attention and talking to her at once. It hadn't occurred to her before just how hard it must be for Hayley. Night and day most likely. Did she ever get any peace from those trying to get in touch with their families through her? Sewing was bad enough with the phone going all the time, but at least she could unplug it. Hayley was at their mercy all the time. It must be relentless. Perhaps they shouldn't mention that Jason fellow. It was probably just to say he'd got a dog stuck indoors without food or something. She didn't like to think of some little dog or cat starving to death or dying of thirst, so she decided to mention it now they were there. It's not like she was asking her to investigate a murder like before. There was definitely no hurry.

Hayley must have given in to one of the spirits on stage as she said, "I've got a gentleman here called Gordon. He's very persuasive and bossy. He wants to talk to his daughter, Margie. Where is Margie?" Abigail and Betty started to feel sorry for Hayley, as it looked like there was no one called that there. "Come on, Margie. Gordon says you're in the third row, second from the end. Everyone turned to look. Tentatively a small mousey woman of about thirty raised her hand and stood up.

"I'm Margie."

"And your dad was Gordon?"

"Yes."

"He says you're still his beautiful little dumpling. And everything is going to be alright from now on; you can tell your mum. She needs to know, and it will cheer her up......Really? Oh that's wonderful. You lost a baby last year, he says, and you don't want to jinx it or get too excited, but your little baby boy will be here in time for Christmas. Congratulations from all of us." The entire audience started to applaud, alive and dead. It was a fabulous moment to end the talk. Tea and homemade cakes were then served as they chatted. Margie told Hayley that she had found out three weeks ago that she was pregnant for the second time but had only shared the news with her husband. She laughed when she said that now everyone knows! There were a few people that said "It must be a fix. I expect she knows her. They just guess half the time." But Hayley and now Abigail knew that there were always those that didn't believe in what you can't see. She was glad she had given Hayley the validation of her gift. Not that she had ever doubted it.

The ghosts and orbs were still buzzing around Hayley and only started to thin out and fade as the Breathers went, the hopes of talking to their friends and family in the audience now passing.

Abigail, Terry, and Betty waited till the hall was empty and Hayley had packed up her notes and equipment before they approached her. Always slowly now. They didn't want to give her a heart attack. They needed her on that side.

"That was amazing, Hayley," Terry told her. "You really put on a great show. You could fill theatres doing that; you'd make a fortune."

"I prefer demonstration rather than show. And I wouldn't have the nerve. I'm not in it for the money. I only ask for a small contribution to keep my website going and that. But thank you, Terry. I feel absolutely exhausted. Everyone wanted a piece of me."

"We didn't realise how hard it can be for you till we saw all those spirits trying to get your attention."

"It can be overwhelming," agreed Hayley. "No doubt you want something as well, Abigail."

"Not at all," she said guiltily. "It's nothing important. It was more a job for Tom actually."

"But you can't have Tom without me, more's the pity. I'm not sure what his hours are this week. What was it?"

"Nothing life and death, you'll be pleased to know. More of a mystery. Maybe a locked-in dog at worst. Terry met this man, who he thinks had been killed in a car crash. He thinks there's something he's got to do or forgotten about. There was no one else in the car with him."

"Where was the accident?"

Terry managed to get a word in. He liked Abigail but she did tend to take over everything. "That he didn't know."

"His address?"

"Not a clue. But I got his name. It's Jason Masters. The accident must have been just outside town on the Gorebridge Road because that's where he came from. I haven't had any word that anything has happened so he must have run off the road. Perhaps Tom could see if there are any skid marks going off or something."

"I'll ask, but I'm not saying he'll have the chance today. I'm sure it can wait till tomorrow."

Hayley walked the short distance to her house and flopped on the sofa after making herself a cup of chamomile tea. Luna meowed till he had been fed, and they both relaxed together. But she couldn't stop thinking about the car crash, so as much as she didn't want to, she eventually decided she had to give Tom a call. She couldn't shake the feeling that this Jason was right. There was something radically wrong.

He answered on the second ring. "You're lucky, I've just finished. I'm getting my uniform off as we speak." Hayley explained the situation and the favour she wanted Tom to do.

"I can remember when you used to ring me to get a loaf of bread and a pint of milk. How I miss those days. Okay then. I'll drive slow. Hopefully, he was going towards Becklesfield as well."

"Do you know, darling, I've got a feeling he was."

. . .

It was not just skid marks in the end that caught Tom's eye but also a broken fence and a flattened hedge. He left his car on the road and ran to see if he could save the driver or any passengers. He may have just been unconscious. One look and he realised that it was too late. The face was pushed up against the shattered windscreen, and his lifeless eyes were staring straight ahead. Regardless, he felt for a pulse in case and checked for anything on him to know who the poor guy was. The young off-duty constable called for help on his mobile.

"RTA on the Gorebridge Road by the turning to Kettle Farm. One male victim - deceased. Navy BMW. Registration - JSM 369. Identification in pocket as Jason Masters. No address. Requesting ambulance and fire brigade."

The ambulance was the first to arrive on the scene, the blue light not needed. The same with the fire engine that arrived ten minutes later. They all agreed that Jason must have been going at 80 mph at least to end up where he did. There were the black skid marks on the road, then the deep ruts on the grass verge and the fence and hedge had been thoroughly demolished. Then to finish the car had slammed into a tree.

"You can see why I called you now," Tom said to the firemen. "He's going to need cutting out. Can you open the boot first? Just need to check it."

"Sure. Here you go……Well, that's a bit worrying, isn't it?"

Tom peered in and saw what was troubling him. "Umm. Duct tape, tablets, and cable ties." He put on a pair of crime scene gloves he always had in his pocket. "Rohypnol. Yep, I'd better ring the station. Johnson's not going to be pleased; he's probably just having his first whisky in the Red Lion about now."

"Who the hell was this bloke? Not a good sign. I'm thinking serial killer," said the fireman.

"I'm beginning to be pleased that Jason Masters is dead, whoever he is. Forensics will have to come as well. See this blanket, there's a lot of long hair on it." He pulled out his mobile phone and walked away from the others. "Serge, we've got a bit of a problem with the RTA I just phoned in. We opened the boot and found something...could be nothing, but there's a bottle of rohypnol, duct tape, and cable ties......yes, that's what I thought......Johnson and Mills?......okay, I'll stay here...... they're just cutting him out now......Yes, I'll wait here for backup, Sir."

The firemen were putting the body of Jason Masters in the ambulance when a car being driven by Sergeant Dave Mills arrived, with an angry-looking DCI Johnson in the passenger seat. He might have known it was Bennett ruining his evening in the pub. And there was a darts match on. "What have we got? You better not be wasting our time, Bennett."

"I hope not, but I thought it should be ruled out. Come and see in the boot, Sir."

Sergeant Mills, who was Johnson's right hand, was a pleas-ant-looking young man and was always smartly dressed - the exact opposite of his boss, whose grey hair grew so fast, it always needed cutting. In contrast, Mills spent a lot of money on his haircuts, something he hadn't given up when Isabella had the baby. They all took a good look. Mills said, "Some long hairs on this blanket as well."

DCI wanted nothing better than for Bennett to get in trouble for time-wasting. "Aye, but it could be his wife's hair on it after a picnic. So on your head be it, Constable. The Chief won't be happy if we call out forensics and make this a crime scene if it's just an accident. Put up the tape, Mills, and get the ball rolling."

Tom received a message back from the number plate check. "Jason Masters. Age 34 of Rook Cottage, Green End Lane."

"We'd better pay a visit to the next of kin." Johnson gave a sly grin. "Don't think you're going home if I can't, Bennett. Follow us. There's nothing more we can do here."

Mills got in the car and punched the address into the satnav. "Eleven minutes, Sir. Blue light?"

"Why not. Sooner we've told them, sooner I can get home." Home? thought Mills. More like pub. Dave Mills had a six-month-old daughter, so he was hoping for an early one too. They were both going to be disappointed.

Chapter 14

TOM COULDN'T DRIVE AS FAST AS THEM, BUT HE STILL managed to be behind them when they turned left into a driveway, lined with hedgerows on either side until they reached Rook Cottage. The gravel scrunched under their feet as they made their way up to the small porch. Nettles and weeds surrounded the path. There was an archway of thorns framing the front door, where once there were roses.

"Right out the way, isn't it? Who'd want to live here?" said Johnson. It certainly didn't look well suited for a young man in a nearly new BMW. It was an old, dilapidated property in serious need of repair. "Perhaps an old gran left it to him." Mills banged the heavy black knocker that was loud enough to wake the dead. "Try again... Right, nobody here. Let's go," said Johnson, as he turned back to the car.

It was starting to get dark, but Tom decided to look around the outside of the cottage. The grass was overgrown, and tiles were missing off the roof he noticed. "There's a light on up there, Sir. And the window's broken. And look here... it's a woman's boot."

"I said it's a dump. Nothing to do with us. Let's go. Uniform can come back tomorrow."

Mills put his hands on his hips. "I think Bennett's right, Sir. That boot looks clean. Something feels wrong, and after what we found in the car, I think we should check it out."

"I'll sit in the car. Bennett, kick the door in. You can explain why."

As the door was in such bad repair, it gave way after two good kicks. They put the light on and had a look around. Inside it was a totally different story. Everything looked new, and nothing was out of place. An all-white kitchen had been added at some point, and it looked like he was tidy to a fault. Whoever Jason Masters was, he was a perfectionist at home, either that or he lived somewhere else, maybe a flat in London, Tom thought.

They went up the stairs to the two bedrooms and a bathroom. Nothing seemed wrong. There was a heavy and long, red curtain against the wall at the end of the landing. Tom pulled it back, expecting to look out of a window, but instead, there was an old wooden staircase leading up to an oak door. Light shone round the edges. More worryingly there was a bolt at the top and bottom. Sergeant Mills and PC Bennett looked at each other, and they both knew exactly what they were going to find. Neither of them felt the need to fetch the boss. Whoever was behind the door didn't need him there.

Mills said they should both put their gloves on, and he pulled back both bolts and slowly opened the creaking door. "Oh my God, it's a girl. Quick."

Tom ran to the bed and felt her neck for a pulse. "She's still alive."

"Ambulance to Rook Cottage, Green End Lane. Near Becklesfield. Woman unconscious but breathing. PDQ."

"I wonder how long she's been here. Miss, can you hear me? We're police. You'll be okay now."

The young girl groaned and tried to push Tom away. "No, it's alright. I'm PC Bennett, and this is Sergeant Mills. An ambulance is on its way. Shall we give her some of this water."

"NO. Don't touch it, Tom. Fingerprints, remember. Let the paramedics see to her. What's your name, Miss?"

"Jessica Green... Miles."

"Did she say miles? Is that a name or has she come a long way? I'd better ring the boss. He's not going to be happy." Mills thought of his own little girl, still a baby. But if anyone had done this to her, he'd track him down and kill him.

Tom held her hand. "An ambulance is coming, Jessica. You're going to be alright. Shall we get her downstairs? It will save time, Dave."

"Good idea. We've got to keep the crime scene clear. We don't want all those feet in here." He got out his phone. "Sir, we've found a girl... No, she's alive...... The ambulance should be here soon...... Okay. I'll see you in a sec." They got Jessica as far as the sofa and laid her down gently. Tom brushed two long strands of dark hair from her face.

"You're okay now, sweetheart. Help's on its way." She was either asleep or unconscious, they weren't sure which. Tom reached for a throw and laid it over her.

DCI Johnson came in and held up a finger to silence them. "Yes, Chief. I had my men enter the property and we found the girl... Thank you, Sir. I know, if I hadn't made that call we could possibly be looking at murder...... Very kind of you... Yes, I'll do the press conference in the morning."

Mills rolled his eyes. "You'll be getting a commendation, will you, Sir?" he said sarcastically.

"I'll mention you too, Sergeant, don't worry." He had no intention of telling them what part Tom had in the case. But he asked him, "How is she?"

"She's freezing, but her pulse is strong. I think she's more dehydrated." He pinched a bit of her skin on her arm and it didn't spring back. "Yes, she is. Shall I see if I can get her to drink some water?"

"A doctor are we now, as well?" But then they heard the siren and saw a blue light. Help had arrived.

It was two in the morning when Tom walked in through the front door. Hayley rushed to the door to meet him. She could see by his face that she had been right to be worried. He had phoned to tell her that he'd found the car and that Traffic were on their way and then there had been no news. But she didn't have to be clairvoyant to know something was wrong.

"Hun, come here. I've been so worried about you. Are you okay?" She held him tight and kissed his cheek. "Come and sit down." Luna woke up and went running over to meet him. He meowed and scratched at his legs until he was picked up and then curled up on Tom's lap. To start with he hadn't wanted 'the bloody cat' as he called it. But now Hayley thought he spent more time stroking and playing with him than she did. And every night, somehow Luna was curled up on the bed next to Tom. She was lucky to get a look in when he was home.

"Get me some tea, please. Actually make it a whisky." She poured one for each of them. "There you go. Now tell me what happened."

"You're never going to believe it. I waited for the fire brigade and ambulance. I thought about what you said about being worried and so we opened the boot."

Hayley put her hands to her mouth. "Not a body?"

"No. But something as bad. Rohypnol, cable ties, and duct tape. The Holy Trinity of serial killers and rapists." Even Hayley hadn't seen that coming. "DCI Johnson and Dave Mills came then and took charge. He just ignored me for making the discovery and wasn't best pleased he had to work when it's opening hours. He's really got it in for me now."

"Take no notice. I have a feeling you'll be his boss soon. Either that or he'll get the sack."

"I wish. So they got the bloke's address from the DVLA - Rook Cottage. That's right out in the sticks." Tom blew out his cheeks.

"Go on, tell me. What did you find?"

"It was an old rundown place. Turns out it was his nan's who had left it to him a few years back. He didn't live there during the week. It was in darkness, so it didn't look like he had a wife and kids, but there was light from a broken window in the attic."

Hayley put her hand on her heart. "What was in there?" she said, fearing the answer.

"A young girl locked in a room. It was the worst thing I've ever seen."

"Just tell me. Was she dead?"

"Nearly. If it hadn't been for you..."

"And you."

"She was barely conscious. We had no idea how long she'd been there. She came round a bit after the paramedics had put a drip in. She was totally dehydrated. They took her to Gorebridge Hospital and she's doing okay. Her name is Jessica, Jessica Green. She kept saying her abductor's name was Miles. But we knew it was Jason. Good job it's been raining lately, the rain dripped through the window she'd broken, so she had a bit to drink. They think the water that was there had been drugged. Clever girl. It broke my heart, Hayley. She had a guardian angel for sure."

"More like Tom Angel. If you hadn't found the car, she'd have been a goner, hun."

"I just wish we could charge the bastard. He's got away with it, hasn't he? DCI Johnson, who is still spitting feathers that I was the one that found the car, is going to do a full forensic search of the house and grounds at first light. He reckons she wasn't the first. There will definitely be evidence of others."

"I'm sure of it, hun. I've got a sixth sense that they should start in the garden. Under the apple tree......"

Chapter 15

Two days later, Hayley went to the library to tell them about the gruesome find, that was exactly where she had said, under the apple tree. Abigail had gone round to see her the previous day to see if they had found the car. She couldn't believe it when she learned what had come to light. The thought that they nearly didn't do anything about it was an awfully scary one for them. Abigail felt the kind of pressure her friend had had for all those years.

Hayley had promised to let them know what the crime scene investigators had found at the property as soon as Tom had told her, even though it was all over the news. The press had been outside Rook Cottage since the news was first released. *Cottage of Hell*, was the headline of one of the tabloids. Luckily Sergeant Mills had been able to get to Mr and Mrs Green before they heard it from elsewhere.

Hayley had rushed to tell the others as soon as she had confirmation that there were other victims. But not until after she had broken down, thinking of what the poor girls had gone through in their last hours on earth.

So with a red nose and blood-shot eyes, Hayley made her

way down a busy Becklesfield High Street to the library. Abigail and Lillian were eagerly waiting for her.

"There were six bodies all together. All of them were buried in shallow graves. He hadn't even bothered to cover them up that well. And there were more than ten different sets of fingerprints in the attic, on the floor and bed. They think there must have been some that didn't report it. They may have been drugged the whole time and he took them back and pushed them out the car. It might all come out now. All those girls that knew they were assaulted but couldn't say, can get some peace of mind now. I reckon there will be a lot more that speak out. And they'll get satisfaction knowing he's dead and can't do it to anyone else."

"I expect some of them and their families would rather he rotted in jail. But at least they don't have to testify in court. How lucky was Jessica. If we don't do anything else, we've saved that poor girl's life. How is Tom? It must have been a real shock for him."

"He hasn't said much, but it really took it out of him. He hardly slept that night and still had to be on duty at eight. Johnson is getting all the credit of course. But the Chief Constable wanted to know who found the car and congratulated Tom. Every little helps."

"I shudder when I think that I nearly ignored Terry and said we shouldn't bother looking into Jason's problem. It shows 'all problems great and small' is a good slogan to abide by," said a shocked Abigail.

"Where is Terry? I was hoping he'd be here."

"He's gone to find Jason and bring him to the library. I can't wait to confront him. I reckon he'll go straight to Hell. If Jim did, he deserves to. It's really upsetting. I've sent Betty and Suzie to take the cat for a walk……Oh yeah, I'm the crazy cat lady as well now!"

· · ·

An arrogant looking young man walked through the large window while Terry followed behind with a face like thunder. Jason Masters did look the perfect man - wealthy and extremely good looking. Just shows you can never go by looks, Abigail whispered to Hayley.

"We've got some news for you, Jason," she started.

"Don't worry about it, babe. I already know. I was there when a chap found the car and opened the boot. It all came flooding back to me then."

"So now you know what you were worried about - the girl in the attic."

"Her? That common little thing? Don't be ridiculous. I was worried about the drugs and cable ties in the boot, stupid. I was thinking I could have got rid of them and hoped she was dead. They couldn't have known for sure it was me then. I only care about Mum and Pops. It's going to be hard for them. She can identify me now and tell the police my MO, as it were. Who knew she'd still be alive days later?"

"Not as clever as you think then. She had the guts to survive, you're just a coward."

"I never walk away from a fight and don't you forget it," he said viciously.

"There's a fight coming for what you've done, Jason Masters, that you can't win. Hell awaits. Your guilt will take you there for all eternity. You're not going to be so tough and cocky then. So don't get too settled here, you scumbag," said a Terry, who Abigail had never seen so angry.

"Guilt? Ah, that's where you and I are different. Between you and me, I feel no guilt whatsoever. Not one bit of remorse. They all fancied me so I gave them a bit of Jason."

"You had to drug them first though, didn't you? You bastard. You'll get your comeuppance," said Hayley.

"You must be the psychic I heard about. You'd better watch

your step. As soon as I can, I'm going to learn how to haunt. I've got a list and you've just been added to it."

"I'm not afraid of you. The devil takes care of its own and you play with fire, you'll get burnt."

"Any more sayings, sweetheart? You just watch your back. Anyway, I would say it's nice to meet you but it's not. And if I'm not mistaken this is my cue to leave. I see a nice young girl. I wonder where she lives. Ciao." He looked at Abigail and winked as he walked away.

"Terry, you've got to do something. There must be some kind of law. He can't just get away with it."

"Have faith, hun," said Hayley. "The Lord works in mysterious ways."

"He sure does," said Terry. "Look."

From the other side of the room a black mist entered. It separated and they saw the spirits of six young women. All looking angry and their haunted, dark eyes focused on just one person - the man that had taken their lives away. The man that had denied them the chance to be married and start a family and live a long and happy life. The hate in them was palpable and as they followed the arrogant Jason out, Abigail almost felt sorry for him. "Vengeance is mine saith the Lord," Abigail said out loud to no one in particular.

After Hayley had left and Betty and Suzie returned with Tiggy, Terry told them what they had missed. They were so relieved that the young girl had survived. Their last investigation with Jim had not been a happy ending but this one was. Abigail was up for a celebration but Lillian had a better idea and said they should all go and visit Jessica in the hospital. She hadn't been there for a few months and for Suzie it was the first time since she had passed. "I think we all want to check that she is alright. It will take years to get over something like that mentally, bless her and it will be nice to put a face to the name. She was our client after all. Even if she didn't know."

They all agreed that this was a marvellous idea, until Abigail thought how far away Gorebridge was when you couldn't just jump in a car. But Terry had that covered.

"The number 8 bus from outside the Post Office. On the hour, every hour."

They even got seats as there were only three pensioners getting onboard, all using their free bus passes. Abigail felt a bit guilty for travelling without paying. But Betty was in her element, she'd been using one for years. Suzie pressed the bell when they got near to the hospital, but the bus driver looked very annoyed at the pensioners when he opened the doors and no one alighted. Old people, he thought. They don't even pay!

Chapter 16

THEY WERE SURPRISED TO SEE SO MANY OF THE PRESS outside the entrance to the hospital. There were two television vans and at least three reporters being filmed and talking into boom microphones. Jessica Green was right; she was going to be famous. Unfortunately, Abigail thought Jason Masters was going to be as well.

Jessica Susan Green, as it said on her chart, was propped up on her pillows and looked very pale. Her long hair, still tangled, had been pulled back into a ponytail. She had various wires attached to her and a drip in the back of her hand. As the press had got hold of the story, she had been given her own room in the private part of Gorebridge Hospital. Her parents and her sister, Holly, who looked just like her, were sitting around the bed. Jessica was trying to smile at them as she could see all of them showed signs of having cried. They had almost collapsed when Sergeant Mills had knocked at the door to tell them what had happened, luckily an hour before they heard it on the television and on social media.

"You're on all the stations and papers, Jess," Holly told her sister. "You always wanted to be famous."

"Not like this," said a croaky Jessica. "Was it on Sky News?" she whispered.

"Yes, I told you. My phone's been going off all morning. Everyone is asking me what happened. Oh and to see how you are, of course. We, I mean you, are going to be rich." Jessica couldn't help but feel that Holly was enjoying this a bit too much. She remembered in her lowest moments she had told herself she might get on television, but now she was safe, it couldn't begin to make up for the horror of it all.

"The police will want to talk to you later, Jess," said her mother, who wouldn't let go of her hand. "They want to know what happened, but I told them not till you're a lot better. That nice Sergeant Mills was so impressed with what you did. He told us you broke the window and didn't drink the water because it was drugged and lived on rainwater you'd collected in the empty bottle. You were so brave, Jess. At least he's dead and can't do it to anyone else. I swear to God, I'm never letting you out of my sight again. You'll have to move back in with me and your dad as soon as you leave here." Jessica groaned at the thought. As if she hadn't gone through enough.

Lillian smiled at her and stroked her hair. She had seen a lot of patients who had suffered trauma when she worked at the hospital, but this was the most harrowing experience she had heard of. But she had the feeling that Jessica would come through it. She had a loving family to lean on. It was just a shame that she wouldn't get her chance to give her side in a court of law. But that was probably for the best. That was for Jessica and her loved ones to know now. And hopefully a counsellor. She had no idea that Jessica was hoping to add a few television personalities to that list.

Lillian thought how strange it was coming back to the place where her life had ended. She looked down at herself - still in her navy blue uniform, clean and crisp as the day she had finished her last shift. Her watch pinned on her chest and two biros in her top pocket. The mud on her flat black shoes was the only thing that would have stopped her from starting her shift on the children's ward.

She looked at Suzie who was smiling kindly at Jessica and listening to the conversation that was going on between parents and child. She never saw any bitterness in her for the good times and love she'd lost. She remembered the day she'd arrived on the trolley. She'd fought death hard after the drunk driver had run her down. But the bang to her head had started meningitis and she had never recovered consciousness. Lillian had stood next to her mother who was holding Suzie's hand and whispered, "Don't worry, I'll look after her until you come," but she hadn't shown any signs of hearing her. And when Suzie took her last breath, Lillian was there to take her hand as she left her earthly body. That was two years ago now, and she would never leave her. Not just because of the promise she had made to her mother, but because she loved her as if she was her own.

She was brought out of her reveries by Holly saying, "They reckon a psychic told the police where you were. She had a vision."

"You're kidding." That will sound good when Piers Morgan interviews me, she thought, before she fell asleep once more. The happy dreams of fame and fortune soon turned into a nightmare where she was lost in a maze with no way out.

Terry called them all over to show them who he had just recognised in the corridor. They felt it was time to leave Jessica to her visitors anyway. Betty decided to do her bit and be a hospital visitor in the geriatric wards. Although she hated that word. She preferred the 'elderly wards'. Geriatric didn't sound friendly at all. Chances were someone she knew was a patient there. When she was alive she had been to one funeral after another in the last few years. In her family, she had been the last one standing. Her youngest sister, Phyllis had died last year, so there was no longer anyone to laugh about childhood fun or remember the hard times. The price of living a long life, she had to admit.

Terry pointed to a serious-looking woman dressed in a pencil skirt and fitted jacket. "See her over there? That is Celia Hanson of the Chiltern Weekly."

"Is she covering the abduction?" asked a nosy Abigail.

"No. I'm sorry to say she's dead."

Abigail felt a pang of jealousy and wasn't sure that she wanted to meet her. Here she was in her pj's and the naturally slim Celia was dressed in a perfectly tailored suit and a shiny bob without a hair out of place. She caught a reflection of herself in a glass door at that point and it did not help at all. Her mum had always said, 'you've got a mass of curls,' when there was a big matted lump at the back, but she was only joking and trying to make her feel better. Then she would gently try and comb it through. How lovely it would be to see her and laugh about her bed-hair once more. She looked at herself from all sides. Shame she'd had that pizza followed by a big slice of carrot cake for her last meal. But apart from the bedclothes and the back of her hair, she actually looked okay. No makeup, which was a shame, but that could have been streaked down her face, so she had to be grateful for small mercies.

"When you've finished admiring yourself can we go and say hello?" said Terry impatiently. Abigail mumbled something under her breath. Honest to goodness, that man could be so grumpy sometimes.

"Hello again, Celia. What brings you here? Are you here to do a story on Jessica? You do know you're dead, right?"

"Haha, Terry. No, I hadn't forgotten. Aren't you going to introduce me to your friends?"

"This is Abigail, a recent newcomer, young Suzie, and this is Lillian."

"You're not Lillian Yin, are you?"

"I am indeed. Have we met before?"

"No. But you're one of the reasons I'm here. Let's go to the staff canteen. There's more room." Luckily, there were plenty of empty tables to choose from.

"Are you The DDA lot that everyone is talking about? I've seen the posters, and then there's a lot of rumours flying around about the Hattons of Chiltern Hall."

Terry managed to speak before Abigail for a change. "Yes, that's us - The Deadly Detective Agency. Were you looking to avail yourself of our excellent services?"

"It had crossed my mind. But it was a complete coincidence that we met here. And it was you, Lillian, I was hoping to meet at some point."

"Now I'm intrigued," she said. "I don't think I can tell you much about anything. Certainly not worthy for a newspaper. I'm probably the most boring of us all. I was a nurse, and then I had a heart attack. Suzie is the best and most important thing that's ever happened to me in two lives."

"Aah, that's where you're wrong. I better start at the beginning, though. Terry will tell you I died about three years ago, and I was a bloody good investigative reporter. My beat was any suspicious deaths, and I used to spend most of my time with the coroners and at inquests in courts. Then I'd follow the obituaries on all the local rags and the one in the Times et cetera. I've got one of those memories that I never forget anything. That's why I was so good at what I did. I didn't have to do shorthand or record my sources. I'd have total recall. So before I died, I heard about a case that was a carbon copy of one that had happened a few years previously, and alarm bells rang. They had both been deemed to be natural death due to myocardial infarction - heart attack, as you well know, Lillian. I went to see my editor, and I told him about the first murder and then the latest one. He told me to run with it but keep it low key for now."

"Fascinating," said Abigail. "What did you find out next?"

"I went to the library and looked at old copies of the Chiltern Weekly."

"I'd forgotten you could do that. It might be handy for us if we get an old case. Sorry, carry on." Terry rolled his eyes. Abigail was really taking charge of everything and never gave anyone else time to speak.

"The first one was a nurse called Doreen Gray. She'd died unexpectedly as she left work at Gorebridge General Hospital. Supposedly a heart attack. She was thirty-eight years old. The only suspicious thing at the autopsy was a tiny pin prick in her back. Otherwise, it was put down to natural causes. You know what I'm going to say, don't you, Lillian?"

"You're wrong."

"The second case I looked into was the death of Registered Nurse Lillian Yin, aged 32. Finished work at eight o'clock and walked to her car in the staff car park. Cause of death - heart attack, with a pin mark in her back. I'm sorry, I really am."

Lillian didn't believe it for a minute. She would have known, she was sure of that. She was a nurse. She knew what a heart attack was like. No, she was wrong. "How do you know it wasn't a coincidence? I'm sure after a twelve-hour shift it's not that unusual. I worked in the children's ward; it could be very stressful."

"I know, you're right. I hope I am wrong."

"That's quite a coincidence," agreed Terry.

"I haven't finished yet. I found out yesterday there was another death. That makes three!"

"Oh for God's sake. I don't know if I want to hear this?" said Lillian.

"Someone needs stopping, Lillian," said Abigail. "We can help Celia."

"Are you sure you're not just excited for your precious Detective Agency, Abigail? You've already taken someone I was falling in love with away. What are you going to do to me now? All because you're enjoying playing sleuth."

"That's an awful thing to say. I would never deliberately hurt you, Lillian. Or anyone. And Jim was a murderer. Did you really want to spend eternity with him?"

"No, of course not. But this looked like fun when we started and now I'm not so sure. I need to get out of here for a while. Come on Suzie, let's go for a walk. I've got to get my head around this and I don't want you hearing anymore."

They both left without speaking. "She didn't mean it, Abigail," said Terry. "It was just the shock making her lash out." He knew she could be bossy and talk over people, but she didn't deserve that. And if the truth be known, before she arrived they were just spirits hovering about, trying to get through eternity. They had a purpose now. You could even say they were righting wrongs. Putting the world to rights, as they say. He hadn't done much in life. Never even got married or had children and till today had never saved anyone's life. But the fact that Jessica was alive and reunited with her family was all down to him and Hayley and Abigail's detective agency. He'd been a bit jealous of her taking all the credit and doing all the talking and making the decisions, but the truth was they needed her and would never have thought of doing it, or dared to. And she was good at it as well. She had the kind of mind that separated the wheat from the chaff. "You've made a difference to all of us. I don't like you to be upset. I'm sure she'll apologise when she comes back."

"I couldn't know that she was going to find this out today, could I?" Abigail felt slightly cheered by the kind words from Terry. She realised it was important that he liked her. Was she getting feelings for him? The age difference seemed to be getting less as well and actually he was rather handsome, she realised.

Celia reassured her that it had nothing to do with her. "Now can I please get on with my story? Thank you. As I was saying, over the years I've often come here to check on things and actually I still sit in on any inquests that sound juicy. I'm looking forward to yours, Abigail. You'll have to come along. Should be very interesting."

"I think I'll pass. They always say eavesdroppers never hear good of themselves. I dread to think what I'd hear. One thing I am going to do is go to Charles Hatton's court case. I want to see him locked up for life. If it wasn't for him, Jim and I would still be living our lives."

The kind thoughts Terry had about Abigail were disappearing again. "Will you shut up and let Celia finish, please!"

"Sorry, I'm sure."

"Where had I got to? So I was here when I bumped into a nurse in casualty. I mean I know when someone is dead. The actual body was in front of us as well. The doctors were shocking the body with those paddles but it was too late."

"How awful to actually see your body being worked on and know that it was useless. I feel for her desperately. And you think she is the third victim?"

"Well, that's the funny thing. It wasn't a woman; it was a man."

"Poor man was in shock as usual. I mean I've seen it all before. I know you're the same, Terry. You try to explain in the easiest and kindest way what's happened."

"He did to me," said Abigail and smiled at him.

"He's very good at it. Better than me actually. I was already wondering if this was the third nurse killing at the hospital, but it threw all the theories I'd had out of the window because I had thought it was a sexual motive more than likely. But after talking to him I have no doubt at all that it's the same killer."

"Tell us about him," said Abigail.

"He's a second-year student. His name is Josh Latham, and he's thirty-four."

"That's a bit old for a student, isn't it?"

"He was a fireman, but he got injured and couldn't do that anymore. He wanted to be a paramedic at first, but then thought he'd had enough of being called out on emergencies. So he had to start from the beginning again and train to be a nurse. He was very good at his job, I've heard since. And patients and doctors all seemed to like him. But I suppose they always say that when someone has died."

"So what makes you so sure it's the same as the others?"

"Three things, Terry. Number one, he was near the end of a long shift in casualty. Two, he had a sudden, unexpected death, and this is the first time I've had actual confirmation - the last thing he remembers is something like a syringe being pushed into his back!"

Chapter 17

LILLIAN WAS REGRETTING ASKING SUZIE TO COME with her. She would have rather been on her own. She didn't want her to see how upset she was. She'd spent the years since they had been together trying to be happy and always cheerful and positive. At that moment, she wasn't just upset; she was angry as well. More than she had ever been in life and certainly in death. How dare someone unknown do this to her. Or maybe not unknown. Could there be a chance that someone who she had spent time with at the hospital had done this? She didn't know which was worse. She had wanted to travel. Maybe even go to Australia to work. One of her friends had done that and loved it. It was going to be hard to ever be at peace now. She felt a pang of regret for taking it out on Abigail. It wasn't her fault, and she was just realising what an awful feeling it was to have been murdered. She had stuck up for Jim against Abigail. She would apologise when she got a chance. It was one thing dying from illness or an accident; that's like an act of God. But some other person just snatching your life for no good reason was such a waste. The promise that she made to Suzie's mother was going to be harder. She didn't want to face her future anymore.

Maybe she should move on and cross over. Suzie would probably be better off without her.

Lillian looked round and saw that Suzie was no longer beside her. She'd walked too fast for her little legs. Suzie asked her to wait up. Not now, Suzie, she thought to herself.

"Don't push me away, Lillian. I want to be here for you. You've done so much for me. Do you know how frightened I would have been if it wasn't for you? How scared I still would be without you? I might still look nine years old, but I'm not a child anymore. I had to grow up fast, and then I've learned and grown with everything I've seen, and that's all down to you. I'm an adult in many ways. Don't you know that we can look after each other now?"

"Oh, Suzie, what would I do without you? I do love you so much. Give me a hug." She knew then that she would keep to her promise. She had Suzie and her friends as well. "Do you want to go and join the others or get back to Tiggy?"

"Tiggy. We can see them tomorrow."

Meanwhile, Betty was doing her rounds of the wards. One of the patients had just passed. Brian, who was in his eighties, had been stuck in a hospital for months and was delighted to be free at last. Betty felt honoured as she was able to witness that his wife was there to meet him, and she got to see both of them passing through the light to what she'd heard described as a 'much better place'. She just didn't want to go herself. Certainly not when the agency was just taking off.

Betty saw the sign for Intensive Care and walked through the closed door. She felt very important as there were two people waiting to be buzzed in. She recognised the lady standing next to one of the beds. Unfortunately, it was the same person that was lying on it. A man, she knew, was her husband, Robert, was sitting and holding her hand in both of his. Betty was a bit confused as the lights on the machine were flashing, and the ECG showed that her heart was still beating.

"Hello, Betty. I didn't expect to see you still here."

"Heather, how are you? Or shouldn't I ask?"

"Well, by the looks of it, not that good, I'd say. I had a kidney infection and an awful pain in my back. Robert rang for the doctor, and of course, they won't come out anymore for a home visit. But he sent a prescription for antibiotics. I went up to bed as the pain was a bit better when I was lying down. I remember Robert called for an ambulance. He said I was hot and talking rubbish, next thing I'm here. The doctor said I was in a coma and the infection had spread."

"I'm so sorry to hear that. At least I went quick," said Betty.

"Your funeral was very nice by the way. Your children did you proud. It was at the crematorium, and then we all went to the Kings Arms. Saved them money, you and John going so close together. It's not often you can have a double funeral."

"I hadn't thought of that."

"I told my kids to do something at home for me or their dad. It's very costly, although we did take out insurance years ago. So they'll be fine."

"But you might not even die yet. Look at poor Robert. He would be devastated without you. If he's anything like John was, he wouldn't know how to sort the rubbish out, let alone work the washing machine."

"But it feels so nice on this side, Betty. It's very relaxing, isn't it?"

"As my old mum said, 'you're a long time dead.' Give it a bit longer; you might as well. This will still be here."

"If you say so, I suppose. I do want to go to my niece's wedding in September. I've got the dress anyway, and look how much weight I've lost. Robert does look sad, doesn't he? I'll have to come back another day."

"Good for you. Bye for now, Heather. If you remember this, tell Robert I said hello."

Her friend disappeared from next to her and Robert called for a nurse not long after.

"I'm sure she blinked a bit. Is that a good sign?"

"That's excellent, and her blood pressure has gone up slightly as well. Both good signs."

Robert smiled and patted his wife's hand. "Come on, Heather love, you can do it."

Betty smiled as she walked away. "All problems great and small," she said to herself.

The following day, a meeting of the DDA was arranged. Although they had said that they wouldn't involve Hayley to give her a break, this was murder. And for all they knew, he or she could be planning another one. Even Hayley would have been annoyed if they had kept it from her. She loved being part of what they did and bringing justice to the victims. So rather than her being sectioned by the librarian, they all met at her house in Church Lane. Celia Hanson, the journalist, was included and delighted to be part of something tangible after the last few years. She had worked so hard all of her life that she had missed the opportunity to do much else. So floating around in a kind of no man's land had bored her stiff. She enjoyed her little pun. That's why she had been a good writer. They needed her as well to give them all the details she had in her head. It was hard to never forget anything. Nice memories were alright, but it was the awful ones that made it so hard. It was bad enough in life.

Abigail opened the meeting and introduced Celia to Hayley. She had noticed on the way over that Lillian was being much nicer to her. She wondered what had brought that on. But whatever the reason it made for a much better atmosphere. God knows, a ghostly atmosphere was frosty at the best of times! And to be honest, Terry had been a bit short with her as well. Suzie had opted to stay with Tiggy at the library. A new book had come in that she had been waiting for.

"So, Hayley," began Abigail. Terry sighed; he had become resigned to playing second fiddle to Abigail. "This is what we've got so far, thanks to Celia. The first nurse - Chief Nurse Doreen Gray was found dead in the car park of Gorebridge Hospital five years ago. It was assumed it was a heart attack. She had a pin mark on her back that they didn't think was important. Then, four years ago, I'm sorry to say, Lillian was found next to her car after a long shift, supposedly a heart attack, again with a pin prick."

"That's when I went to my boss about an exclusive, so I started digging but died before the inquest," Celia added.

Betty had an idea. "Is it just me? Or does anyone else find that a bit suspicious as well? You start looking into it and then die?"

"Good point. Yes, how did you die, hun?"

Celia shook her head. "No, don't worry. It was a multi-vehicle pile-up on the motorway on a rainy night. I wasn't the only one. I even went to my inquest and there was nothing fishy."

"Thank goodness," said Betty. "We've got quite enough murders for one case."

"We should keep an open mind. You may have been getting too close to the truth. Whoever it is, they have already got away with three murders," Lillian pointed out.

"Only two so far. Hopefully, the police will look into this one."

"Tell me about the last nurse, Celia," said Hayley.

"His name is Josh Latham. A second year student. He's 34. He was in the fire brigade and retrained when he got injured at work. I'm not sure how. Perhaps we could find out in case it has a bearing on things. He was going to the pharmacy at work and he fell down the stairs."

"Well, that's a totally different MO," said Terry, frowning.

"I know. But what about him feeling a syringe in his back? It can't be a coincidence. Are you saying a man who had gone into burning buildings couldn't walk down a flight of stairs?"

"Were there any witnesses?"

"No. But the pharmacy is on the lower level of the hospital, so it's a good place to choose if you want to kill someone."

"It would have looked like a heart attack if he hadn't fallen down the stairs. Maybe he didn't have a chance to wait till Josh had finished work," agreed Abigail. "So, in order, it's Doreen Gray, Lillian Yin, sorry, Lillian, and now Josh Latham. Had you come up with any suspects, Celia?"

"I had, but I'm not sure now that the last one is a male. The first suspect is Doctor Douglas Gibson, and he was seeing Doreen Gray or another Sister at the time, so the rumour went. He's a cardiologist, and he's worked there for about twenty years, so he would have known them all. Although I can't say for sure. He's known as a bit of a ladies' man. I've heard he's had numerous affairs."

Lillian raised her hand. "Well, talking for myself. I knew him. He thinks he's God's gift to everyone, not just women. He used to do the rounds when he wasn't seeing out-patients. He was good, so I'm surprised he's not a consultant at a private clinic by now. He was very arrogant and didn't really mix with the nurses unless he fancied them. We were just there to do what he said. Saying that though, one Christmas party he let his guard down and got a bit flirty and handsy. I think actually I might have gone out with him once or twice. But the next day he was back to his normal stuck-up self."

Betty said, "And being a cardiologist he would know how to make a death look like a heart attack. He'd know exactly what drugs would work."

"That's very true. Anyone else?" asked Abigail.

"Well, don't laugh. But the janitor, Adams, looks very, very dodgy. Some of the nurses feel uncomfortable around him. Again though, this was before a man was killed."

"It's always the janitor or the butler," said Betty.

"Jack Adams was the one that found the body, and he's coming up to retirement soon. Maybe he wanted to do one more killing. Or he felt that they had more success than him or earned more. Jack Adams was working there before the first murder, and his work room is on that floor."

"So he could be a witness or a suspect. It's too late for witnesses for the other murders. But we need to check for this one," said Terry. "Any more?"

"Just one. Lillian, do you remember Matron Bright?"

"Do I? She trained me. The original battle-axe. Can't believe she's still there. She seemed old then. The real spinster, married to her job type. But I think there was a rumour of her having an affair with a doctor. She never did like me, but she wasn't very nice to anyone. Unless you were a doctor."

"Yes, she's still there. Now she had a run-in with Sister Gray. As Sisters, they were both up for the Matron job which was given to Doreen Gray first off. So when she died Bright naturally got the post. But I can't think of a motive for the others. Unless she got a taste for killing. Nurses have before. But it's usually killing their patients. They like having the power of life and death, but it's very unusual, I must admit. We need to find out how the others got on with her," added Celia.

"We're going to need her alibi for the day that Josh fell. And the others. Another idea is a disgruntled patient. Perhaps they hadn't got the treatment they wanted or a loved one had died while under their care," said Abigail.

"I would have thought they would have gone after the doctor," said Terry. She always had good ideas, blast her.

Hayley did a round-up. "So we've got a Doctor Gibson,

Matron Bright, a Scooby-Doo janitor, or a thousand-plus patients. We should see if anyone filed a lawsuit before Doreen Gray died. What else, Abi?"

"Hmm. Well, if Terry is in agreement," she said diplomatically, which was unusual for her, "Celia and Suzie could look at the newspapers on that archive thingy back at the library to see what it says about the deaths and any court cases. You'd better wait till it closes though. And I'm wondering if Josh Latham will still be at the hospital. Betty and Lillian, could you go and find him? He'll talk to you two. Take him to the staff canteen. If he's ready to leave, we could do with him at the library. But it's up to him. I think he'll stay where he feels at home. See if he knows any of the suspects or has heard of the other murders. They must be connected."

"They are," said Hayley. "I feel it but not how. While you're there, check out the janitor. See what he gets up to and who he talks to. What about me, Terry and you?"

Abigail sat up. "We've got to talk to Tom."

"Oh no. I was hoping we could do it without him. He's still at work and he's not going to like it."

"I know. But all he's got to do is get us the paper files on the two oldest murders. Didn't you say he wanted to study for his sergeant's exam? He could say he's researching old cases. And if we solve the murders of three nurses he'll get the credit. None of us can say our part in it. You can't either, Hayley."

Celia added, "If you were found out, Hayley, there would be at least thirty journalists camped outside. Believe me, I know."

"With the other cases, Johnson said it was down to his fantastic leadership that they were solved, so I don't know why he's worried. It puts up his success rate. Tom had to say it was an anonymous tip for Charles Hatton and just luck he found that smashed car. The Chief Constable has got a soft spot for Tom since he found that little boy that was missing at the fayre, and he doesn't like DCI Johnson one bit. He's too old school for the new force. Totally tactless and says it how it is. And scruffy. His bosses hate that. Tom won't get off duty till eight tonight though."

"That's fine. Don't worry, Terry and I will wait." The others all said their goodbyes and left.

"Actually, Hayley, while we have time, I know I've known you for years but you've never told me how you got into this paranormal stuff."

"I'd love to hear about that too, Hayley. I've heard it runs in families," said Terry.

"My gran always said my mum was fey. But I didn't know what that meant for years. She never talked to me about it. But the first I knew about it was one night Grandad came and sat on the edge of my bed and told me that he loved me and to tell mum that he was alright. So in the morning I went into Mum and Dad's room and said why didn't they tell me Grandad was staying and they said that I must have dreamed it. But a couple of hours later they got a call to say that he had passed away that night. I think I was about six or seven."

"That is so interesting. I've gone all goosebumpy," said Abigail. "What else did you see?"

"Different people off and on. I'd be going down the road, and my eyes would lock with someone, and they'd look at me kind of surprised, and I knew they were gone. But I'd look away quickly. Sometimes I couldn't get rid of them; they'd bombard me with questions or things they wanted me to do. Even follow me home, so I learned how to ignore the feelings. Before Mum died she told me that she did the same. It was only as living people asked me for help that I thought perhaps I could help them and do some good."

"And now you can't get rid of us," laughed Terry.

"Tell me about it. But somehow it's different. You've helped me to do a lot of good. And I'm so grateful that you've finally proved to Tom that I'm not nuts or making it up."

"Did he really used to think that?" asked Abigail.

"Not as such. It was more denial, if I'm honest. We met at school, you know. Not exactly childhood sweethearts as we met again a few years after we had both left."

"Did you find it hard at school, being the weird kid?"

"Not at all. You would think so, but they were all kind of impressed with me 'seeing dead people'. And some of them wanted me to tell them their future. I only guessed but mostly I was right, luckily."

"I have a feeling it wasn't luck," said Abigail.

"Maybe not. So Tom knew I had this gift or whatever but he wasn't that interested. I mean there were a few times when I made him listen. We were going somewhere once, and I had this awful feeling that we shouldn't. I think it was driving to see his cousin, Karen, in Surrey. You might even remember; that was the day when that plane crashed on the dual carriageway. We would have been there at the same time."

"That's amazing, Hayley? So what did Tom have to say to that?"

"Not a lot. He'd just joined the police force then and the last thing he needed was for the others to find out he'd got this psycho psychic wife. So I didn't mention it much. He knew I started doing readings for people, but I never asked for payment, only a donation if they wanted to. I had to have money, didn't I?"

"Course you did. You shouldn't feel guilty about it," said Terry kindly.

"I know, but I do. So the only time I talked to Tom about it was when I felt something about one of his cases."

"Like the jewellery you found in that barn?"

"Yes. Obviously it's different now. I still think he'd rather not know but..."

"We haven't given him any choice," added Abigail guiltily.

"But we make such a good team. I promise not to bug him from now on."

"I'm sure he'll be glad to hear it. But sorry, hun," Hayley put her fingers to her temples, "I have a strong premonition that you don't mean that for a minute!"

"I meant to ask you," said Terry, "Did you get the address of that poor woman who is being haunted?"

"Oh yes, Janette. I totally forgot to mention it with all the talk of these murders. She lives at 43, Windmill Lane."

"I know it. It's one of the old cottages that used to house the workers. We'll go the next free night we have, won't we, Abigail?"

"The sooner the better. That poor woman is being scared to death. I keep thinking if that was my old nan who was going through that, I'd go mad. I think just Terry and I ought to go, so we don't scare her ourselves. We'll sort it out and let you know how our ghost surveillance goes."

Chapter 18

Suzie and Celia waited until the last person had gone and the librarian had locked up. Then they found the newspaper archive thingy, as Abigail had called it. They started with the Chiltern Weekly.

"It's so frustrating I can't help, Suzie. Doreen Gray died in July 2018, so go back a few months and see if you can see if anyone died or sued the hospital or a particular doctor."

"Okay. I'll have a go." It was a long process, but in the end, they found something.

Celia pointed to the screen. "Gorebridge General Hospital was sued by the parents of Molly Soames. Thirteen-year-old Molly was sent home twice with suspected headaches, which was later found to be a brain aneurysm. The parents settled out of court for an undisclosed sum."

"They might have been paid, but that doesn't make up for a lost child. My mum would still want revenge."

"We'll have to see if Hayley could talk to them perhaps. But why kill a nurse? It's the doctors that make that kind of decision, surely."

Suzie agreed. "Let's see if the murders are in here."

"I checked when I was alive. There was a bit in the obituary about Doreen Gray, but nothing about Lillian. I can't wait till the next issue comes out to see if Josh's death is in there. Surely my boss will have connected it by now. Hang on a minute. I've had a great idea, Suzie. Let's go back to where I worked at the paper and see if there's any pointers to see how they are covering it."

It took them about half an hour to get there, and then they had to wait till Oliver Pickett, the editor, went home. Celia had forgotten the long hours that they all had to put in to get the paper out on time.

Celia could only stand and watch as Suzie moved the sheets of paper around. But near the top was a sheet with the typed words 'The sad news that a nurse has died in an accident at Gorebridge Hospital'. Oliver had clipped a handwritten note on it, 'Look into this - re Celia Hanson. Number 3?'

"Thank goodness. I knew he wouldn't let me down. Can we leave a note and tell him he's right?"

"I could but he wouldn't see it, I'm afraid. I might be able to write it on a computer if you know how to turn it on."

Celia sighed. "If I can guess his password maybe. Press this to turn it on. Try Chelsea. I know he supports them."

"No. Not Chelsea."

"His daughter is Debbie. No, not Debbie. His wife is Linda. No, not her. His dog! Oh God, what was it? He brought it in when it was a puppy. It was one of those sausage dogs. Ummm. Banger - that was it! Try Banger one."

"Yay, well done. We're in."

"Click on notes and write this - Josh Latham was the 3rd nurse. Look into Dr Douglas Gibson. Jack Adams the janitor. Chief Nurse Michelle Bright. George and Sadie Soames, parents of Molly. Then sign it, Yours Celia Hanson. That will freak him out!"

.   .   .

At 8.30 am, when the editor of the Chiltern Weekly turned on his computer, he was very shocked to see a list of names, supposedly from his best reporter. He called security to see who had broken in and used his computer at 9.34 last night. They found the CCTV for that time and sent it to him. He couldn't believe it when he saw the light turn on and no one was there. And the office chair turned on its own just as his computer screen lit up. Oliver, ever the professional, took it in his stride. Perhaps there was something in these rumours he'd been hearing about, that there was a spiritualist helping the police. His own wife had been at a WI meeting and there was one there that she'd been raving about. He wrote another note to add to the other one - Look into Police/Medium.

He picked up the phone to speak to Celia's replacement. "Liam, get in here, will you. I've got some names I want you to check. There's going to be a wonderful exclusive."

He wouldn't ask the police for any comment yet. He wanted to get all his ducks in a row.

He silently thanked Celia, but then shivered. "It's very nice of you to help, but please stay away!"

Chapter 19

"I'M SO SORRY, JOSH," SAID BETTY. "YOU HAVE OUR condolences." Lillian and Betty had found him eventually in the cardiac ward.

"Not as sorry as I am. I'd just started over. Newly divorced and a new girlfriend. Luckily I didn't have kids or else I'd be really mad. If it was natural causes I would have been alright with that, you know, if your time's up so be it, but I'm really fired up now."

"I know how you feel. I've just found out I was murdered by the same person. According to Celia, anyhow."

Josh frowned. "Are you sure she's right?"

"That's what we've got to find out. If I was, it doesn't necessarily mean you were, and vice versa. I was on my way to my car after a shift and never got there. What do you remember?"

"I had to go to the pharmacy, and I hated waiting for lifts, so I went down the back stairs. I remember a feeling like I'd been stung in my back and then falling. That's about it. That other woman said I wasn't stung; it was a needle jabbed in me."

"That's why she thinks it's the same killer. There are a few suspects. A Doctor Gibson. Do you know him?"

"The cardiologist? Yes, of course. He was looking at a heart attack patient of mine, Mrs. Timms. He's okay. Hardly spoke to me. I'm just a lowly trainee to him. Who else?"

Betty told him. "It's a matron. Michelle Bright. And the caretaker, Jack Adams, was there when you died."

Josh puffed out his cheeks. "Chief Nurse Bright is scary. And I could see her hitting someone on the head with a baseball bat but not a stab in the back. But I guess you never know. And old Adams? He's a bit weird if I'm honest. I mean I wouldn't want to see him out of work or anything. Creepy, I suppose, is a better word. But I haven't even spoken to him, so why would he want to kill me?" Probably for that reason, thought Betty. Getting on a bit herself, she often felt ignored by the youngsters. You became a bit invisible over the age of sixty.

Lillian asked him if he had ever heard of a lawsuit for a wrongful death, but he said it didn't ring a bell. They told him about the newly-formed Deadly Detective Agency and invited him to come to the Becklesfield Public Library when he felt he could face the outside world again.

"Where would we find Jack Adams? Will he be here?" asked Betty.

"Yes, if he's not changing a bulb or fixing something, he'll be downstairs, on the first level. I'll show you. And you can see where I fell. It's right by his room."

Josh left them to it, and they passed through the janitor's door. It was a mess with plenty of black bags and bottles on shelves. They heard him outside the door, rattling the keys to get in. They grabbed each other and started to giggle. "What are we worrying about, he can't see us," said Lillian.

A grumpy-looking man with grizzled hair and beard walked in. He was carrying a carrier bag. "Do you think he's got a head in there?"

"Or a dead cat. He does look like a mass murderer, actually. I wonder if he's married," said Betty.

"Doubt it. He's probably buried her under the floorboards," joked Lillian. Just then, his mobile phone rang, and they both jumped a foot in the air. Jack Adams answered it, and they saw the screen showing a picture of a little girl.

"Hello, Grandad." A smile broke across Jack's face. "Hello, my little angel. What are you up to today?"

"Me and Mummy are in the garden watering the beans that you planted for us. They're huge."

"Of course they are. They've got to be big enough for Jack to get to the top. Tell Daddy I will be around later to help him with the fence and read you a story."

"Mummy says see you later. Bye, Grandad."

"Bye, Poppy. Love you."

Betty had tears in her eyes. "Well, that shows us, doesn't it. That murderer Jason Masters had the face of an angel, and you know what he was like. I feel a bit guilty now."

"Just because he loves his family doesn't mean he couldn't kill someone else. But I agree," said Lillian. "All those years that I worked here, I didn't speak to him or say hello. I wish I had. Perhaps Hayley could talk to him."

"At the very least, we need to stop anyone arresting him for murder!"

Constable Tom Bennett was sitting at his desk when he got the phone call from Hayley. What did she want now? As he thought - more information. He was due to finish at eight, which meant if he wasn't called out on a job, he had a while to think of an excuse to go to Records and get the files. It was in the basement, and he would not normally have an excuse to go there. He could have downloaded the information off his computer, but there would be a record of that. DCI Johnson would love a reason to sack him for improper use. But it had helped last time Hayley had asked. They arrested a murderer and found a body.

That Abigail seemed to know her stuff, just a pity she was dead. She would have made a great policewoman. He looked around. No one was looking at him. Johnson and Sergeant Mills were interviewing a local thug, Matthew McKinley. He had taken a machete to another well-known felon, Duncan Sanders. He had changed his statement when they showed him the attack was on CCTV. It had started with them talking and then arguing. He said it was over a woman. Duncan had hit him first, and so he went to his car and got out the machete. Sanders never stood a chance. He better get a move on before they finish. He had heard McKinley wanted to get out of there fast and be taken to remand. Something about his cell being haunted.

It didn't take Tom long to run down the stairs two at a time. WPC Jane Nichols was in there finding a file as well. He exchanged a few words with her and then she left. He looked at the scrap of paper he had jotted the names on - Doreen Gray and Lillian Yin. The last name he seemed to know. "Where have I heard that name before?"

He shoved both files up his navy jumper and stopped by his locker and put them under his clothes. Luckily there was no one else in there.

He went back to his desk, whistling, but then stopped when he realised it made him look guilty as he had never whistled before at work.

"Got nothing to do, Bennett? You sound far too happy," Inspector Johnson threw some papers at him. "Here, type Matthew McKinley's statement out."

"Yes, Sir." That was a close call. This is the last time ever, Hayley!

Hayley got to the front door before Tom had a chance to get his key out. "Hi, hun. Give me a kiss. Now come in quick. We have company, Tom, so best behaviour."

"That's great, Hayley. Just what I want when I get home from work late at night. Who is it this time?"

"We have Abigail and Terry, so play nice."

"Hiya. Well, I nearly got caught today, so this is the last time."

Abigail told Hayley to tell him that he will thank them when he catches a serial killer.

"A serial killer? It's got to be three or more to be that."

"This is only the start, Tom. There's one, maybe two more. And they've all been at the hospital, and for all we know, this could be happening at other hospitals. Could be why there have been gaps in between, if the killer was an agency worker or a visitor at other ones."

"Don't you think you're getting a bit carried away?"

Terry told Hayley to tell him that they might be able to do a DNA test now.

"They will only do that if they think it's murder. Let me look at them first, and then you can tell me why you think it is murder," replied Tom. Luna, who was meowing for attention, finally got picked up and settled on his dad's lap.

Abigail got very impatient while he was reading and couldn't keep still. Death was boring sometimes. You couldn't just go and put the kettle on, she reasoned. At last, he put the files on the table and looked at Hayley. "Well?" she asked.

"I see nothing that says it's anything other than heart attacks. The first one, Doreen Gray, finished work, left the building, and was found deceased by a visitor, Tony Pearce, at 6.14 pm. No signs of a struggle. Same for your friend, Lillian Yin. Again, she had done a ten-hour shift and was found next to her car by a nurse, Stephanie Epsom, at eight something. Both heart attacks. And yes, there were pin marks, but they couldn't conclude anything from that. There won't be anything I can do to open either of the cases. Even if it turns out that Josh Latham's death wasn't an accident, I don't think they will connect it to these two. I'm sorry, darling, but this time you and your little band of sleuths will have to give it a miss."

"Good morning. Is this the Chief Constable?"

"George Carson, yes. Who's this?"

"Oliver Pickett. Chief Editor of the Chiltern Weekly."

"What can I do for you, Oliver?" Carson knew he had to keep the press on his side.

"Do you know anything about a serial killer killing nurses at Gorebridge General Hospital?"

Carson gave a nervous laugh. "No, of course not. I think we would have noticed. What makes you think we have one?"

"Before she died, one of my reporters was looking into it. There were only two then, but now there has been another suspicious death. A young nurse, called Josh Latham."

"I can assure you if there was any truth to this story, my detectives would have been on it. Of course, now you've brought it to my attention, I will see if there's anything in what you say. Can you email the names and dates, Oliver?"

"I'll do it now. And while I've got you, is there any truth in the rumour that a medium has been helping with some cases? Apparently, that was the reason Jessica Green was found at that cottage, and I heard they even had a hand in the Hatton arrest."

"Now that I know is untrue. We just use good old-fashioned police work here, Oliver." He had heard about a psychic, but not from his officers. His wife had told him about a medium who gave a talk to her Women's Institute group. "She's marvellous, George, and although her name is Hayley Moon, I happen to know she's married to your PC Bennett. You should use her on your cases." He did like to keep Mrs Carson happy; she could be very forceful if not. It did seem odd that Masters' car had been found, and a few other cases had been helped by his input. If it helped with the regional arrest numbers, it couldn't hurt either.

Might be worth keeping an eye on young Tom and bring him in on a few more cases.

He had a sudden thought. "I take it you won't be printing anything about any of this. Can you imagine the panic if you say people are being killed at our hospital?"

"Not people - nurses."

"Exactly. That sounds even worse, and I'm sure you've got it wrong. But leave it with me, Oliver. Bye." Chief Carson clenched his fists and picked up the phone again. "Get me DCI Johnson. NOW."

Chapter 20

Hayley was very surprised when Tom rang her from work the next day about the case.

"You'll never guess what, Hayl. I've been put on the nurses' case. I've been assigned to help Mills and Johnson. We're going to the hospital in a bit. How the hell did you manage that?"

"Fantastic, hun. I'm so pleased for you. It's nothing to do with me, though."

"Apparently the Chief said he wanted to open the case and insisted I should help. Asked for me by name. As you can imagine, Johnson is spitting feathers. Got to go, talk later."

This definitely warranted a visit to the library. If only Abigail had a mobile, was her last thought as she grabbed her jacket and went out the door.

Sergeant Mills and PC Bennett drove the short distance to the Gorebridge General Hospital in the same police car. DCI Johnson preferred to go in his own. It was easier to go straight to the pub after work, was the consensus of most of the station.

They waited for him in the carpark and watched as he drove in and parked in one of the four disabled spots.

"With me, Bennett. Time you learnt some proper police work from the best. Mills, you go and interview the staff that were there the day Latham died. So last Thursday at about twoish in the afternoon. See if you can find that caretaker, Adams. He's an unsavoury character according to some, and he found the body, remember. We'll take the other two on the list - Doctor Gibson and Matron……"

"Bright, Sir, and they aren't called matrons anymore," said Tom helpfully.

"I know, boy," snapped Johnson. "You just take the notes and keep your trap shut. You're only here because the brass wants it. God knows why. I don't even know why we're wasting our time with all this. Someone killing nurses? Give me a break. And find out who sent Latham down to the pharmacy, Mills. See you later."

"Very good, Sir." Mills went off to find HR to see who was working with Nurse Latham in the Emergency Room last week. They printed him off a list and highlighted those that were working there that day. It didn't include the doctors or ancillary staff that were there at different times. Luckily, all five nurses on the list were on duty again, so he followed the signs to get their statements.

Tom and the DCI were shown to Doctor Gibson's office and were told he was with a patient, but Johnson just walked in. "You can't come in here, whoever you are," shouted the doctor, who had his stethoscope on an elderly man's chest.

"DCI Johnson, Gorebridge CID. We'll give you five minutes," and he shut the door again. "Think they're Gods, that's the trouble with doctors."

Tom was beginning to think that Johnson didn't like anyone,

man or woman. He had heard his wife had left him many years ago, and he wouldn't have blamed her.

"Find a machine and get me a coffee - two sugars." But the patient came out and gave them a hard look. Johnson didn't wait to be asked and walked in.

"Will this take long? I've got patients all afternoon. What do you want anyway?"

"Your name has come up in a murder enquiry, Sir."

Doctor Gibson was not expecting that. "Don't be so ridiculous. I'm a doctor; I save lives, not take them."

"Nevertheless, a male nurse died in suspicious circumstances last week. A Josh Latham fell down the stairs when......"

"What was suspicious about that? As you say he fell, and I didn't even know him. Do you know how many nurses work here? You're a fool if you think I had anything to do with it."

Johnson did not take kindly to being called a fool. "If you don't want to be dragged down to the station, I suggest you tell me where you were last Thursday around two o'clock."

He shook his head and looked at the diary on his computer. "Well, I was here that day. I was at out-patients in the morning and then my rounds of the cardiac ward. After that, I could have been called anywhere. I finished at three thirty. It would be up to you to check where I was about that time. You'd need to check with each department's records of the patients that I treated. Shouldn't take you more than a few hours."

Johnson gave a sly smile. "Don't worry, the young PC here would love to do that. So you don't think you know the nurse. Show him the picture, Constable." Luckily, Tom had taken a picture of Latham from his driving licence on his phone.

"Not that I can remember. There's more male nurses than you'd think these days, Inspector."

"One more thing, doctor, do you remember Nurses Doreen Gray and Lillian Yin? They died here as well."

"That was years ago, and again I might have known them by sight or on the wards, but that was all. Do I need to say that I am very friendly with your Superintendent?"

"You can say what you want, but it won't help you. This comes from above him. You might want to call a lawyer, Sir." Johnson was enjoying himself. He was working class, born and bred, and hated the 'don't you know who I am?' brigade. "Well, that's all for now. Don't leave town without telling us. We might need you to come in and make a formal statement."

DCI Johnson stood up to go but looked daggers at Tom as he asked, "Just one thing, Sir, are you ever asked to go to the ER to see a patient?"

"Er, yes. If it's a cardiac emergency, or they need me to make an assessment for surgery."

"What about last Thursday?"

"I don't think so. Not that I remember. But as I say, it's up to you to find out, isn't it?" Was it Tom's imagination or was the good doctor lying?

"Right, we better go and see this Matron."

"Chief Nurse, Sir."

"In my day, you knew where you were. You had the matron, and the other nurses did what she said or she put the fear of God in them. Same as the police nowadays. No respect. And what did I say about you talking?"

"Keep my trap shut, Sir."

"Remember that next time then. Now go get me that coffee," he bellowed.

A nurse pointed out where they could find Michelle Bright and she led them to an empty treatment room. "What's this about, Inspector?"

"Detective Chief Inspector Johnson. We want to talk about the death of Josh Latham last week."

"An awful tragedy. He had so much potential to be a fantastic nurse, and he was so good with the patients. Everybody liked him. He was older than the other trainees, but that didn't matter at all."

"He was a fireman, wasn't he?" asked Tom. "Sorry, Sir."

"Yes. He was injured on the job. It wasn't anything that would stop him nursing. If I remember correctly, he suffered damage to his lungs from smoke inhalation. Poor man."

Johnson asked, "So do you know what happened? Were you here that day?"

"I was. I usually work Monday to Friday. I've done an investigation into it, but obviously there will be a proper inquiry here at the hospital so it doesn't happen again. But I understand he was on his way to the pharmacy to fill a prescription for two elderly patients. It was a busy day, and once they had their tablets, they could go home. They weren't going to be admitted. Rather than take the lift, Nurse Latham ran down the back stairs, and being in a hurry, he fell. Sad, but not suspicious, I wouldn't have said."

"That's not up to you, though, is it? And where were you at the time, Nurse?"

"Chief Nurse. Really, Inspector, well, I certainly wasn't pushing one of my nurses down the stairs, and it's up to you to prove that I wasn't."

"Do you remember Doreen Gray?" The change of subject shocked her.

"Of course I do. She was a dear friend. Why?"

"What about Lillian Yin?"

"I haven't heard those names for a long time. Lillian I knew quite well. Why are you asking about them? They died of heart attacks, surely."

"We are not at all sure of that anymore. That will be all for now. We might need you to make a formal statement, ma'am. So don't go away anywhere."

. . .

Once outside, the DCI said, "I'd love that old bat to be guilty, but I don't know why she's on the list. Or that doctor. Carson just said it had come to his attention. I've no idea what's going on. It wasn't your wife, was it, Bennett?" he said and burst out laughing."

"Haha, very droll, Sir." He gave a wry smile and thought if he only knew...

Sergeant Mills was also wondering what was going on. He had been told to only ask about the last death, but he had been told about the other two. And why had Bennett joined them all of a sudden? He thought he had got help from somewhere, but he wasn't bothered. If he could rise to the top on someone's coat-tails, he wasn't worried. Maybe the boy was just lucky. Although he had heard that his wife was some kind of psychic that had helped sometimes but mainly it was just a rumour. Johnson hated Bennett enough already and that wouldn't help. He thought he had shown him up over the kidnapping. Mills hoped that one day in the future he'd be the DCI, and Tom could be his sergeant. Perhaps Isabella could invite the Bennetts for dinner. The mother-in-law could babysit for one night.

It was hectic in the emergency room when he got there, but he managed to talk to the nurses one by one. He started with the older one who was in charge. She wasn't on duty last Thursday, but Mills decided to ask if she remembered Doreen Gray.

"Yes, I remember Doreen. It was so sad when she died. And unexpected. She was so happy to get that promotion to Chief Nurse as well. Perhaps that was why she had that massive heart attack."

"I heard Michelle Bright was hoping to get that?"

"She was as mad as a wet hen. Mind you, the rumour that

she'd been having an affair with Doctor Gibson didn't help. She blamed Doreen for starting it. He wasn't best pleased either, nor his wife. Neither of them shed a tear when she died. Karma, Michelle reckoned. So she got the job after all and that was that. Why do you ask? I thought you were here about Nurse Latham?"

"Oh yes, I am. Someone just mentioned her name, that's all. Is it okay if I ask some of the others about him? I won't keep them long."

"If you can do it without disturbing the patients, please, Sergeant."

They were all devastated by the death of their friend and colleague. One of them, Nurse Pitt, had been with Josh before he fell and was probably the last one to see him alive.

"I worked with him a lot that day, and I remember thinking I wish I had been the one that had been asked to go to the pharmacy. I really needed a break from the bedlam and I would have loved an excuse to get out of here. Children were crying, and earlier an old man had died after a fall. It was one of those days."

"So you were there when he went to fetch the tablets?"

"Yes. There were two ladies who were discharged, but they needed their pills before they could go home in the ambulance. It made sense to get them out so there would be two more cubicles free for the next ones. Some were in the corridor on trolleys by then. Same as today."

"Is it usual to ask a nurse to go, rather than say someone at reception?"

"It's better if the patient can go, or a helper, but that's not always possible. But it does happen."

"I don't suppose you can remember who actually asked him to go, can you?"

"Umm...it was Doctor Gibson, that's right."

"Thank you very much, Nurse. You've been very helpful

indeed. One more thing, could you show me the way he would have gone?"

"Anything to have a break. Sister, I've got to show the policeman the way to the pharmacy."

"Don't be long then."

She smiled at Tom and said, "No, Sister. Josh could have got the lift down, but he didn't, obviously. So he'd have gone this way." Nurse Pitt showed him to a door that was in need of a coat of paint. "Patients don't usually come through here because it's not signposted. But they could if they knew the way. It's not private or anything. This is where he fell."

There were a lot of scuff marks on the wall and on the grey stairs. Mills would need to get a team here to take fingerprints, but a week had passed and it must have been cleaned many times. Although not all cleaners would do the walls as well as the rails. They went to the bottom together. Nurse Pitt was in no hurry to get back to work and was enjoying being part of the investigation.

"This is where they found him. No blood but then he had a head injury, I heard. Poor Josh."

"Do you know the man that found him, Jack Adams?"

"The caretaker guy? Yes, I know him. Not to talk to of course. He keeps to himself and he's a bit creepy if you ask me."

"He works down here, doesn't he?"

"His office and stuff is down here, but he works all over doing odd jobs. Would you like me to show you?" she said eagerly.

Tom laughed. "No, you'd better get back, Nurse, sorry. But thank you for your help."

"Glad to. You know where to find me," she added, as she walked reluctantly back up the stairs. He could see the pharmacy at the end of the corridor by the lifts, but where he was seemed to be Jack Adam's domain. There was the entrance to the boiler room, a room marked Caretaker, and a large storage cupboard. Mills was surprised that it wasn't locked as it was full of cleaning products and things like lightbulbs. He knocked on Adam's door and entered. He was standing at a work desk with a pair of pliers in his hand.

"Can I help you? You're not allowed in here."

"Sergeant Mills, Sir. We're doing a follow-up to the death of the nurse that fell, Josh Latham."

"Yes, I know. I found him. Was too late though."

"Was he still breathing by then or maybe he said something?"

"I'm not a medical man, but even I know when someone is dead. His eyes were open and he weren't moving. So I went for help. Ran up the stairs and stopped the first person I saw, which happened to be a nurse. She went off and brought that Bright woman back."

"Was she nearby then?"

"Musta been. She was only gone for half a minute. I think she was coming out of the ER. So she went down and more or less took over. I carried on doing what I was going to do before. Why do you want to know? He fell as sure as eggs."

"More than likely, but we have to check these things. Had you met him before?"

"Might have seen him around, but I can't say I take much notice. I don't bother them and they don't bother me. I retire soon anyhow, thank the Lord."

"Do you mind if I have a look around while I'm here?"

"Can I stop you?"

Mills smiled at the old man. "No, probably not, Sir." He opened a few cupboards that were full of tools and looked on the untidy desk. He opened the drawers that were jam-packed with wires, knobs, and all sorts of random things. Bit like our kitchen drawer, thought Mills. The one on the bottom left was a bit stiff, and thought it might have been locked but a hard pull and it opened. He gave a sigh; he had really hoped he wouldn't find anything. The old boy reminded him of his grandad - grumpy but wouldn't hurt a fly. In there were packages of bandages, plasters, scissors, and at the very bottom was an opened box of syringes. Apparently, they had all been jabbed in their backs.

So he had to do the very thing he didn't want to - he got out his mobile and called Johnson.

Chapter 21

"So Johnson arrested poor Mr Adams, did he?" said Betty. "That is so unfair. I know he's an odd fish, but he wouldn't kill anyone."

An emergency meeting was made that evening so they could hear what had happened on Tom's first day in the CID. He was making himself scarce in the kitchen, cooking himself egg and chips. It wasn't much fun living in a haunted house and was even more unnerving to hear your wife talking to herself all the time. She'd told him that Betty, Lillian, and Abigail were visiting.

"Tom said he took him into custody after they bagged the syringes and the other stuff for evidence. Jack said he only had them because they had been thrown away and it was a real waste. The syringes were all individually packed and were still in date. By all accounts, he's a right hoarder, so his wife says. He keeps everything. Every piece of wire left over, every nut and bolt and even the boxes that they come in. She's sitting at the station now. She might as well go home for the night."

"What about the others? Bright and Gibson?" asked Abigail.

"Doctor Gibson said he hardly knew Doreen Gray, but

Sergeant Mills found out that she'd spread a rumour about him and Bright having an affair to make sure she got the job, so he's obviously lying. You wouldn't forget that in a hurry, especially as his wife found out. And he didn't admit to sending Josh to the pharmacy either. Trouble is, he knows the Superintendent, so he's not going to accuse him without being sure."

"But he can arrest Adams. Why does he think it's him?" asked Betty.

Hayley shrugged her shoulders. "Apparently, he says he's got the means and the opportunity and he's just making up the motive and he was actually at the hospital for the other deaths. Says he's retiring and wants to do one more murder. Absolute rubbish, I reckon."

Lillian added, "He might have had syringes but no way would he have known what to put in them to make it look like a heart attack. I'm a trained nurse, and I wouldn't have a clue."

Hayley shouted out to Tom, "Lillian says how would he know what to put in a syringe? She's a nurse and she wouldn't know. Say that to Johnson."

"Johnson said he could have grabbed something from the pharmacy at any time and got lucky. Poor old boy is totally bemused. I feel so sorry for him. Mills tried to tell him to hold off, but he knows best."

"Betty says will they let him go tonight as there's no smoking dagger?"

That tickled Tom. Hayley said she had a way of mixing up her metaphors, but said that was part of her charm. Out of them all, she was the one he would have liked to meet. Abigail seemed a bit on the pushy side. "I think they might have to. There's no real proof yet, so make sure you lot work it out. The whole station would love to see him with egg on his face."

"Abi wants me to go and see the Soames family to rule them out. I might even be able to help them. I was going to go in the morning if that is okay?"

"They're at the bottom of Johnson's list so I'm sure that's fine. He thinks he's solved it anyway, so go tomorrow but keep your phone on in case we turn up and you need to get out fast." Tom sat down at the kitchen table to eat his tea in peace, apart from Luna rubbing against his legs for a cuddle.

"What shall we do tomorrow, Abigail?" asked Lillian.

She thought hard. "Me and you could go to the hospital. Hopefully, Josh will still be there. I've got some questions for him."

"I think he will be. If not, I know where he lives - lived. What about you, Betty? Do you want to come?"

"I think I'll spend some time with Terry. I haven't really seen him much since... well..."

"Since I've come," said Abigail. "I hope he doesn't resent me."

Lillian said, "He did call you the sergeant major the other day, but I think he was joking."

Betty went over and patted her arm. "Take no notice, dear. You're just what my mum would call a bit on the bossy side."

"Thank you, Betty, I think. I have no idea why he would say that, it's so unfair. So we'll meet back here for a mission briefing at eighteen hundred hours tomorrow!"

Hayley was not looking forward to seeing the Soames, and she just hoped that Molly's mother would be on her own. Men could get very angry when she told them who she was, and she hadn't worked out what she was going to say yet. It was the best part of eight years since their only child had died, and walking up the path to the front door she wondered, should she go as Hayley Bennett or Hayley Moon? Just Hayley, she decided.

Mrs Soames opened the door with a little boy standing next to her. "Can I help you?"

"I know this is a bit unusual, but I wanted to say how sorry I was about your daughter's passing."

She hadn't been expecting that, and her smile quickly disappeared. "That was a long time ago now."

"I know, but I recently lost someone myself." Her friend Abi had died, and she wasn't exactly lost, she thought, but it was only a small white lie.

"Come in then. My husband doesn't like to talk about it. Even my friends never want to mention my Molly to me. I'd enjoy a chat about her. As you can see, we've had another child, but that doesn't take away what happened, although it helps. Please sit down."

Hayley couldn't help but look at all the pictures around the room. There were a few of her son, but most of them were of a beautiful girl with curly hair and a cheeky smile.

"She was very pretty."

"And bright. They said she could have gone to university. Are you a counsellor or something?" asked Mrs Soames.

"Of a sort. I'm a sensitive and feel things. I often work for the bereaved. And don't worry, I'm not asking for any money before you ask. Like I can tell you are unsure of me and thinking I wish she'd go away. But if it helps you to trust me a bit, there's a lady here in a green cardigan. Her name is Julie."

"My nan. You must have looked it up, that's all."

"She says you are looking after the azalea bush well."

That made her eyes widen. "How did you know about that? We dug it up last year from her house and planted it here. Ask her if Molly is with her, please."

"She's not here but she said she is fine and only worries for you and her dad. And she is so happy that you have got Jamie now. Julie told me his name. She likes the name because her husband was James and that's near enough. Tell me about Molly, Mrs Soames."

"She was beautiful inside and out. We taught her right from

wrong, and although she was a teenager, she never caused us any worries. As good as gold. Too good to live, some said."

"I can believe that, bless her."

"Would you like a cup of tea, sorry, what's your name?"

"Hayley, and I would love one."

In Gorebridge, Abigail had managed to track down Celia Hanson to meet her and Lillian at the hospital. The journalist knew more about this case than anyone. Not for the first time, Abigail wished she was wearing a smart business suit like she was, rather than pyjamas. Even Lillian looked nice in her navy nurse's uniform.

"Hello again. I haven't found Josh yet; he's not in the ER," said Celia. Lillian asked some of the Deads that she knew were wandering around, and they suggested looking where he had died.

"Apparently, Josh hangs around at the top of the stairs trying to recreate how he fell or if he was pushed."

"Such a shame. Let's hope we can give him closure soon," said Celia.

They found him at the bottom of the stairs and persuaded him to join them in the staff canteen. It was quite empty as it was another hour to lunchtime.

Abigail started the conversation. "How are you, Josh, and has anything come back to you?"

"No, nothing. I remember being at the top, and then I felt a pain in my back and fell forward."

"Did you hear anything? The door opening or did someone say anything?" asked Celia. "If you were pushed, they would have had to come through that door. You would have noticed them if they were coming down from the floor above."

"I know. The more I go over it, the more confusing it gets. Have you learned anything at all?"

"Well, they arrested Jack Adams."

"That old bloke? Oh, for goodness' sake. Why would he do it?"

"Why would anyone? He wouldn't have wanted to kill me either, Josh," said Lillian. "He retires soon, and from what Betty and I heard, all he wants to do is sit in his garden and spend time with his granddaughter. He'd never jeopardise that."

"Let's think of some reasons for who wanted you out of the way, Josh. That's how we started when we were working out why anyone would want me dead," said Abigail.

Lillian laughed and said, "Yes, but that was easy - annoying, nosy, bad jokes..."

"Bossy," added Celia.

"Haha, very funny. Don't listen to them, Josh. It actually could have been jealousy, money, love. No, don't laugh, you lot. Have you seen anything you shouldn't have?"

"Well, it wouldn't have been love. I've just got divorced, and that was mutual, and I haven't been with Melony for long, so there's no one else in the picture, no exes or anything. I can't think of any enemies. As a fireman, I might have had a few run-ins with people, but not enough for murder. What did it turn out to be for you then, Abigail?"

"I saw a photograph that I shouldn't have, and I was killed for that. And it didn't even register with me. So he needn't have bothered. What could you have seen lately, say on that day?"

"It was literally a normal day. I got up, and my girlfriend dropped me off on her way to work at about eight. We didn't get into any road rage or anything. It was a normal shift in the ER. Busy like always. After lunch, it got even more hectic. The waiting time had got to about four hours. There were angry people, but there always are, and I can't say I blame them. One old man had fallen and died in front of us, but he came in by ambulance, so he didn't wait that long, and his sister was upset but not homicidal. There were a few children who needed X-rays, and I wheeled them down. A few heart attacks."

Lillian had an idea. "Did Doctor Johnson get called to those?"

"Yes. He came to see one of the old ladies, but he said she could go home, and that's why he asked me to go to the pharmacy, and there was a prescription for another woman."

"He was on my list with a motive, but I can't think of any reason for killing you," said Celia. "Also, the difference with you is that the others were all on their way home. Lillian and Doreen were both in the carpark. You were the only one inside and not after a long shift."

Abigail had a thought. "Which might mean that he or she was desperate and had to work fast before you could do or say something. I think we might be getting somewhere. Now, you were found by Jack Adams, and Doreen was found by a visitor. Celia, who found Lillian? Celia has got an eidetic memory and she can't forget anything. Which I should imagine is a curse and a blessing."

Celia looked up to the ceiling. "Another nurse who was also on her way home - Stephanie Epsom. She performed CPR, but Lillian died soon after."

"Oh, bless her. I didn't know that. I wish I could thank her."

"She left a few years ago. Early retirement to look after a relative."

"I kind of remember her. She was getting on a bit then," said Lillian.

Celia looked up again and closed her eyes. "You finished at eight and went to your car. She saw you on the ground by your car and did CPR as you were still breathing at that point. A Doctor Pearce came over and pronounced you dead at eight nineteen, so she stopped. She was a very good nurse, apparently, and had been here for years. They all spoke highly of her when I checked into her. Did you know her, Josh?"

"Who was it again, Epsom? The name rings a bell definitely, but I can't say I know her, but maybe."

"She worked in the geriatric ward."

"I was due to go there next after my stint in the ER."

Lillian said, "That's where I know her from. I was working there before I got the job in charge of the children's ward, my dream job. I loved it. That's why I love looking after Suzie."

"My dream job was being a fireman. I would still be doing it now if it wasn't for my chest."

"Did you save a lot of lives and carry people down ladders in the middle of the night?" asked Abigail. "I bet you did."

"I had my hero moments. But mostly it was mundane stuff like small fires, accidents..."

"Cats up trees and saucepans stuck on kids' heads?"

"I can honestly say that I never had to rescue a cat stuck up a tree. A child once, yes. In my opinion, cats have got more sense. I'm going to miss those days. Even going to miss the excitement of nursing. I was pretty good at it, even if I do say it myself."

Lillian told him, "I know it's not much consolation, but everyone I've spoken to here has only good things to say about you. Patients and staff. Even Bright told Tom what a good nurse you were apparently."

"Thanks, Lillian. One thing I want to know though, knowing what the hospital is like, is if you had finished a shift and went out the door to the carpark, how come your shoes are muddy?"

"How could I have missed that?" exclaimed Abigail. "Great catch, Josh. I thought when I first saw you that Matron would have been after you in the old days. But it's easy to get used to things, isn't it? Come on, let's go to the carpark and look. I expect it's the same."

They went outside to do a reenactment. "I would have come out of this door after my shift, and I always parked over there on the left. I can't actually remember, but I usually did." There was a grassy area on that side that separated the car park from the maternity block.

Abigail looked puzzled. "That's the only place where you could have got mud on your shoes. Would there have been any reason for you to have gone over there, Lillian?"

"No. If it had been to do with work, I would have gone out the main exit and used the path to get there. I was definitely on my way home. Unless I saw someone I knew and went to talk to them. But I can't think of who would be there for the life of me."

"And it was," joked Abigail. She really must stop herself with the puns. "But hang on, there might be another scenario. You might have been chased over there, and you doubled back to your car and tried to get inside, away from whoever was after you."

Lillian closed her eyes. "I'm glad I can't remember then; I must have been terrified. It's like in a horror film when they are trying to get their keys in the door but they can't. Please, Abigail, I know we've had our differences, but I really hope you figure this one out."

Abigail went over and took her hands and gave her a quick hug. "We'll get there, all of us together. In fact, I've just had a thought. I don't want to speak too soon, but I've already got the beginning of an idea. I may be wrong though, so I need to get Suzie to help me look up a few things in the library after clos-ing. But I think you saw someone, Josh. Someone who was worried that you recognised them, and it had to do with one of the past murders."

Lillian wanted to know straightaway. "Which murder? Mine or Doreen's?"

"None of them," Abigail said and knitted her eyebrows together while deep in thought.

"Then whose? There's no one else."

"I'm pretty sure it was yours, Celia."

Chapter 22

At six o'clock, the librarian showed the last person out of the library, locked the door, and left herself. She hated being on her own and felt like someone was watching her. On that particular night, it was Abigail, Suzie and a small ginger cat called Tiggy.

The others had gone ahead to Hayley's for a meeting. Abigail said she would join them as soon as she could. First, she needed Suzie to look up some births and deaths, and if they found those, then a newspaper article and the electoral roll. She just hoped she was right. She would look so stupid if she was wrong.

Suzie decided not to go to Hayley's but stay with Tiggy and finish her book. Since Abigail had arrived, she had really grown to enjoy all the Inspector mysteries and the Murders in the wherever. She could never work out whodunnit, unlike Abigail. Suzie thought she was just wonderful.

Over at Hayley's, she was not quite as popular. "Abigail has no more idea of who has done it than the man on the moon," Terry was telling them. "And now she keeps us waiting for her big denouement like she's the great detective in a novel."

Betty didn't like to hear that kind of talk. She liked Abigail very much. "She's just checking something in the library, and then she'll be here. I'm so excited." She was sitting with Lillian and Terry on the sofa. Celia was in one armchair, and Hayley in the other. Josh didn't want to miss the outcome, and he had arrived with Lillian and was pacing up and down. Luckily, Tom was still at work. Hayley hated it when Tom kept asking what they were saying all the time. She would phone him or tell him what happened when he got home. She felt a sudden whoosh of cold air.

"Sorry I'm late, everyone. I hope I didn't miss anything."

"We wouldn't start without you," said Betty. Abigail caught Terry rolling his eyes but decided to ignore him this time. He nearly laughed instead when he saw she was standing in front of the fireplace like Hercule Poirot. "Lillian said you might know who the killer is. I can't believe it. You are so clever," added Betty.

"I don't know for sure yet. First, we need to hear what everyone has found out today. How did you get on at the Soames' house, Hayley?"

"I loved Mrs. Soames; she was really lovely. I didn't meet her husband, but I'm sure they would never kill anyone. They brought Molly up with strong morals and taught her right from wrong, so they wouldn't have gone against their beliefs. Especially not in Molly's name. And they have got a beautiful little boy now as well. Actually, I had a lovely chat with her, and I think I gave her some peace that she needed."

"I have no doubt about that, Hayley. You're amazing at what you do."

"Thanks, hun. I haven't got anything else myself, but I've had some updates from Tom. Unfortunately, Johnson is going to charge poor old Jack Adams, bless him. Sergeant Mills thinks it's simply to close the case and get the CC off his back. And then he'll get shot of Tom as well and send him back on patrol. Plus, Doctor Gibson has put in a complaint to the Super about the way he was spoken to, so he wants it wrapped up. He's going to hold a press conference tomorrow. If it wasn't for the fact it would ruin Jack's life, I'd let him go ahead and announce it to the world, and then Tom could tell him he's wrong in front of everyone. But we'd better not. So if we can solve it tonight, I'll get Tom to tell Mills to break the bad news to him. Now, Abigail, we're all excited to hear what you've come up with, and we're amazed because Lillian said you think Josh was killed because he knew something about the person who killed Celia."

"I love that you have faith in me, but actually, I don't think it was a person but a them!"

Terry exploded at the statement. "Oh come on! For God's sake, Abigail." He couldn't keep quiet for a second longer. "I don't believe for a minute that you know anything. You just like to be important. The centre of attention."

Abigail felt such a fool. Not only for thinking they had faith in her, but also as she had begun to look at Terry in a new way recently. She thought they had got closer after they saved that poor girl, and he had even stuck up for her after Lillian had had a go at her. She had started to care for him, and he was only ten years older than her, and time and years meant nothing anymore to any of them. When will she ever learn? Never probably.

"I'm sorry you feel like that, Terry. I have noticed sometimes you resent me and don't think I haven't seen you tutting or laughing behind my back. So I'll tell you what I think happened, and if I'm right or if I'm wrong, I'll leave you in peace. I'll move on. The detective agency was a bad idea, I see it now. It's turned all your lives, well, you know what I mean, upside down." The room fell silent.

Betty was the first one to speak. "I love the agency, Abigail and so want to hear what you have to say."

"Okay. I'll finish what I was going to say, and then you can agree or disagree."

"Yes, please," said Celia. "Let's go back to where you said Josh was killed because he knew something about my murder. But I'm not sure I agree. It was an accident on the M1, on a very wet road. I know from the inquest that I braked hard when a lorry slowed down and I went into him and a car went in the back of me and then another one into them. The motorway was blocked for hours, and it was deemed an accident. Fortunately, I was the only one that died, but there were five other people who were rushed to the hospital with some serious life-changing injuries."

Abigail took up the story. "But out of all the murders, yours is the only one that Josh could be linked to. And it wasn't because he was a nurse. Unlike the others, it was because he was a fireman.

You had to be got rid of because you were looking into the other murders and had gone to your boss to do an exclusive in the paper. You'd interviewed an awful lot of people at the hospital, and you know how these things get about. The only person that would have been worried about it would have been the murderer.

Of course, it would have to look like an accident. Your editor would have been even more keen to run a story if your death followed that pattern. No, you couldn't have a heart attack. This one had to be a random accident. How easy would it be to follow you on a busy wet road and when they saw you brake, they would literally run into you while accelerating? It turned out even better because you were in between them and a lorry. Unfortunately for them, the car behind them was travelling too close and went into them as well. Josh, you were a fireman, I daresay you saw a lot of cases like this. I know when Tom found

Jason Masters' car that had crashed into a tree, he called an ambulance and the fire brigade. He had to be cut out, as I remember."

"That's right. It was a big part of the job."

"And tell me, Josh," Terry thought, she thinks she's in court now. "About two years ago, were you called to a multi-car pile-up on the M1, where at least three cars had gone into the back of a lorry, with one fatality?"

"Oh my God, Abigail, I was. There were two cars we had to cut open."

Abigail gave a bow and said, "I rest my case, M'Lord," to Terry.

Chapter 23

"WELL, I'M BLOWED," SAID CELIA. "THAT IS AMAZING. You really have a flair for this. What a shame you're dead."

"I know, it's so annoying. All dressed up and nowhere to go."

"Well, not that dressed up," laughed Betty. "But you still haven't told us the where, why, and who. I'd die of excitement if I hadn't already."

"How on earth did you work it out?" asked Lillian. "I heard everything you did, and I'm none the wiser."

"All of you and Tom gave me the information, and I kept the important stuff in my pocket for later." Abigail looked down at her pyjamas. "Well, my hypothetical pocket, obviously. And anything that seemed to not fit, I tried to remember somewhere else."

"Under your hat," added Betty helpfully.

"Exactly. There were a few things that stuck out like Sister Gray and Bright falling out over a promotion, and Lillian had just been promoted to the Children's Ward. What were the chances of Celia just happening to die at that time? Pretty slim, I reckon. Then there seemed no motive for Josh to have been killed unless it was something else. And knowing what I was killed for made me think long and hard about what Josh could have witnessed. But the biggest clue, or actually discrepancy, was to do with your death, Lillian. Someone told a lie. I would have missed it if you hadn't shown me. I couldn't have got there without you."

"I'm glad to help, but I've absolutely no idea how I did."

"It was right in front of me. At first, I thought the murders were because you were women and it was love or jealousy. So it could have been an outsider or someone in the hospital, but when Josh was killed, it blew that theory. But after I had worked out who it could be, the rest fell into place. I realised the actual motive was because they were nurses, but not for what they were but because of what had happened at work. Lillian, you had just got your dream job in the Children's ward. Doreen had just been made Chief Nurse, or Matron as it was in the good old days."

"So it was Michelle Bright, because she wanted that job like a ......" said Lillian.

"Folks don't kill for a job," growled Terry.

"Terry, you and I know that people kill for a lot less. But no, it wasn't Bright because she got the job and wouldn't have killed for your job, Lillian. No offence."

"Don't forget I hadn't been promoted, Abigail," said Josh.

"No. I still think you were killed for knowing something."

"So tell us about the clue and how I helped," said Lillian. "Because I haven't got a clue."

"Luckily for us, our new colleague has an eidetic memory and could tell us exactly what was said at your inquest. Down to the exact names and times. And Josh reminded us about your muddy shoes, which we had all got used to and thought no more about. We had been talking about the fact that poor old Jack had been the one to find you, Josh, and then we talked about who found you, Lillian.

Celia told us that a nurse, Stephanie Epsom, finished work

just after you and found you unconscious by your car. She gave you CPR, but you died just as Dr Pearce arrived. As they do, he called time of death at 8.19 pm. Well, Lillian got very upset as we were talking about it. It can be a profound, upsetting place where you died, I know that. So I gave her a hug, and that was the pivotal moment for me."

"I don't get it." Josh said what they were all thinking.

"I got close enough to see her fob watch! Remember, Terry, you told me Jason's fancy gold watch stopped working at the moment he died. Well, the doctor said she died at 8.19, but what does the watch say?"

Lillian got up and walked to the mirror above the fireplace. "Twenty past ten."

"No, actually it doesn't. You look, Josh. Don't forget you have to lift up a nurse's chest watch to tell the time, and a mirror turns it the other way as well."

Josh went over and tilted his head to see it. "She's right, you know. Just before ten past. About 8.09."

"Oh my goodness. It's been pinned to my uniform for years, and I can only see it in a mirror, and it looks like twenty past ten!"

Abigail took up the story again. "Oh yes, so it does. But we all missed it, like the muddy shoes. I forget I'm in pyjamas sometimes. It's amazing what becomes the norm. She said you were still alive when she found you. So who was lying? I doubt it was the doctor; he hadn't been there. So the only one that could be lying was the nurse that had been stuck on the geriatric ward for 25 years - Sister Stephanie Epsom.

I think she followed Lillian out of the door, and perhaps you saw the syringe and probably the look on her face and tried to get away. I think you ran on the grass and then struggled to get in your car, but she caught you. She had to take the syringe out and put it in her bag, but then, and I can only guess, she saw the doctor coming and knelt down by you and pretended you were still alive and told him that you were still breathing. That's when he took your pulse and pronounced you dead at 8.19."

"And it's all because of a promotion that I lost my life?"

"I'm afraid so. It must have built up after a life of disappointments. She'd worked there all her working life. Stuck on the same ward and never considered good enough for promotion. You see, she was one of the old-fashioned nurses that had never been to college. She'd learned on the job, and that wasn't what the hospital wanted anymore. She'd given everything to her job, and any chance of a personal life had passed away. I think she turned bitter and hated everyone, including herself."

"But she left years ago. To look after her brother who was disabled," Celia reminded her.

"Josh said he could remember the name Epsom but not Stephanie, so that's one of the things Suzie and I looked up in the library. Remember he said that an old man had died of a fall on the day he died and his sister was there. We looked up to see if Stephanie had a brother. She did. A brother six years older, called Lewis. And when we looked at the deaths for last week, lo and behold, a Lewis Epsom died at Gorebridge General after falling down the stairs."

"I remember now. His name was Lewis Epsom. His sister was upset but said she was used to death as she used to be a nurse. I even told her that I used to be a fireman."

"That sealed your fate, I'm afraid. She must have recognised you from the day of the accident. And before you say anything, Terry, the other thing we looked up was a page in The Chiltern Weekly, from three years ago, where it says 'Their very own, much respected reporter Celia Hanson was killed in a car crash.' It also listed the survivors and that Lewis Epsom had been left with life-changing injuries. After that, she retired and looked after him. Suzie checked the electoral roll for me and she had been living with him all her life."

"Why would he have wanted to help her?"

"That I wouldn't know, but I'm thinking that she didn't drive and if she didn't drive, why was she in the car park at all? She needed him to do it. Perhaps she told him if he didn't help her she would go to jail and then he'd be on his own. She's obviously a psychopath so who knows what hold she had over him. The day he died, she must have worried that you recognised her from the accident that had killed Celia Hanson, who had been investigating nurses' killings. Perhaps with Lewis dying she thought you might be able to connect her to the death. It was common knowledge around the hospital that nurses should take care when they left work and that Celia Hanson thought there was something going on before she died."

"I would never have put that all together."

"Trouble is, she's like Charles was with me. They are very similar people. Both are narcissists so they think the world revolves around them, and they are so important we're sure to be fixated on them."

Terry added, "If she did kill Josh…if…how come she had the syringe and poison with her? She wouldn't know she would meet him, would she?"

"Good point. But her brother died in the morning and the electoral roll had their address, and it's literally half an hour's walk from the hospital. I think she went home and grabbed it. Then all she had to do was hover around till Josh had finished his shift. But luckily for her, she watched him go to the pharmacy and took her chance."

"If it's true, how are we going to catch her? She's not going to admit to it, is she?" said Terry.

Hayley had an idea. "I could visit and tell her that Lewis has come to me and she has to give herself up."

"No way, Hayley. That's far too dangerous. She's already killed four people that we know of. And do you know what, I wouldn't be surprised if she killed her brother. Who knows, she might have pushed him down the stairs, especially if he was threatening to come clean. I think you need to tell Tom what we think and maybe Sergeant Mills could tell Johnson."

"Oh my goodness, hun. Can you imagine what he'll say? He'll go bananas. Do you think they will get the proof, Abigail?"

"It's a lot easier when you know who you are looking at. They'll probably find the poison in her house or her fingerprints or DNA in the stairwell even. The police can check when Lewis got to the hospital and someone might have even seen her watching you, Josh, and following you out. As for the accident, the police will have a report and can find out who was driving the car that went into you, Celia. If she was in the passenger seat or driving, that alone would be suspicious. What would be the chance of her ramming in the back of someone who was investigating a murder that she was connected to? Then they can check her alibis or work schedule for the other murders. Failing that, I'm sure DCI Johnson will be able to bully a confession out of her."

"Serves her right, I say," said Lillian. "Such a waste of lives. I feel really depressed now. I wish we could all go to the pub."

Celia clapped her hands. "Nonsense, we should all be happy. The Deadly Detective Agency has just solved two cold cases and one or maybe two more murders. God knows who else Stephanie Epsom would have killed next."

"I do," said Abigail. "I think she might have gone after Hayley. She had visited the Soames and she might have gone on to see any of the other suspects. Terry is right, I'm awful for putting you in danger."

"No, I didn't say that. You're bossy, self-opinionated, loud..."

"But?"

"There's no but..." said Terry and smiled. "But, actually you're pretty amazing. I take back all I've said. Well not all, but most."

"Thank you, Terry. It was a joint effort, though. And Celia, we couldn't have done it without you. Let's hope the paper will do an exclusive when it all comes out, and Hayley, you can get Tom to tell them to mention Celia."

"The thing I'd like most is to help your detective agency from time to time."

They all agreed to that and chatted for the next ten minutes until Hayley put a stop to it.

"Now as much as I love you all, please could you go and haunt someone else for a while. Luna needs feeding, and Tom will be home any minute and I think it will be a lot easier and definitely quicker if you weren't here."

"I know, Terry. While we're on a roll, why don't we visit that Janette in Windmill Lane, who's being haunted day and night?" suggested Abigail.

"I know how she feels," laughed Hayley.

Chapter 24

TERRY AND ABIGAIL WAITED OUTSIDE JANETTE'S house until they were sure she had gone to bed. The last thing they wanted to do was scare her to death. As Terry had thought, it was one of the cottages that the farmers were given with the job, in the days when the workers and their families had to doff their caps to the Lord and Lady of the manor. And if they didn't, they could lose their jobs and the tied house, same as if they were too sick or too old to work, they'd be out. He couldn't quite remember how he knew all these things about the four cottages in front of him, but they brought back some new memories for Terry, and he couldn't help but wonder why. And they were not very good ones for some reason. No wonder Janette could feel an atmosphere, even though now, these small terraced houses were worth a small fortune, and no farmer he had known would ever be able to afford one.

"Are you okay, Terry? You look a bit worried."

"I've got a funny feeling that I've been here before, Abi. That I lived here, but I know that I was brought up in an orphanage for as long as I can remember."

"Maybe it was before you can remember, then. Like when you were under five."

"Could be. For some reason, I know that the main bedroom is at the front and the little one is at the back…and the fireplace in the parlour…I can remember the surround was made up of squares of bricks. Three bricks going across and three bricks going vertically, so it was like a chequered pattern."

Abigail took his hand and said, "Let's go and see."

They crept in quietly; even Abigail managed not to speak while she followed Terry to the parlour. She pointed excitedly to the fireplace that was exactly as Terry had remembered - squares of patterned bricks. Terry just gave her the thumbs up, and they started to check the house, looking in each room for anything odd and at one point hiding behind the sofa, but they didn't see any ghosts. Janette had a bookcase full of mystery and horror books. Maybe she was scaring herself and just paranoid.

Upstairs in her bedroom, Janette was huddled down in her bed and looked to be very restless. She had made sure it was very light in there as she had left the landing light on with the door open, but she didn't get up or hear anything while they were there. They stayed hiding in the shadows for about two hours and then decided to give up and whispered that they would try the following night. Terry, who knew about these things, didn't feel any residual energy like there would usually be after a haunting. Perhaps she was imagining it, reading one of the many horror books wouldn't help. But they owed it to Hayley to keep on with it.

Neither would admit to it, but it was rather nice that it was just the two of them, as they never had the chance to be alone these days. It was strange that he found her really annoying sometimes, yet he missed her when she wasn't there. He never had these conundrums when he was alive as he had been the original bachelor. It felt confusing but rather nice, so yes, they would definitely both have to return another night - for Janette's sake, of course. And Abigail promised to help him unravel the mystery of his knowing all about the house, that he had never been in!

In the Gorebridge CID office, everyone was walking on eggshells around DCI Johnson. He had been about to give his press conference about the charges against Jack Adams with the television cameras starting to roll when Sergeant Mills said he needed to have an urgent word with him.

After that, it soon got around that he had arrested the wrong person and the culprit was a little old woman who lived with her brother. Most of the station thought it was hilarious and no less than he deserved. Mills and Bennett hovered close to his door hoping to hear what he said to the Chief Constable who had just telephoned him. After five minutes, they rushed away as it flew open, and a very irate Johnson bellowed, "Mills, Bennett, with me, NOW. Get me the address of this Epsom woman. Why the hell wasn't I told about her before? Heads are going to roll for this, mark my words. And if I find out you have anything to do with this, Bennett, you'll be working nights in the roughest part of Gorebridge for the next ten years."

"Interview starting on May 22nd at 11.15am. Detective Chief Inspector Johnson and Sergeant Mills are present, with the defendant's solicitor." They were sitting opposite a middle-aged man, in a pinstriped suit, and a thin, upright woman with a smile on her face, who looked a lot older than her sixty years. Like she wouldn't hurt a fly, thought Mills.

"Please state your name for the tape."

"Stephanie Anne Epsom."

"Stephanie Epsom, you've been arrested for the murder of Nurse Josh Latham and Celia Hanson and possibly others, even your own brother. What have you got to say?"

"Not guilty, of course. I didn't even know either of them, and you can't prove I did."

"We know you met Nurse Josh Latham at the hospital on the morning of May 11th when your brother died."

"I met a lot of nurses that day. They were very kind to me. But I was so broken-hearted over my brother's death that I can't remember any of them, Inspector."

"If you say so. We also have witnesses that saw you come back to the hospital later on that day."

"As I said, I was very upset and now that I think about it, I went back to see if I could collect his personal things. Also to try and find out what had happened. I had every right to be there."

"We made a search of your house and found syringes, Miss Epsom. Autopsies are being done to see if either of the victims had been given anything suspicious."

"I was a nurse who cared for my disabled brother, so I naturally had syringes."

"We found the drug Entrinatron at your house. If we find a trace in Josh Latham or your brother, we've got you. Then we'll exhume Doreen Gray. Unluckily for you, she was buried, not cremated. We also have evidence that your brother was driving the car, with you as a passenger that killed Celia Hanson - the journalist looking into the nurses' killings."

"I never met her."

"She was doing an article and had been asking questions at the hospital while you were still working there. I'm sure someone will have seen her talking to you or that you saw her. You weren't that popular, were you, Miss Epsom? Passed over for all the plum jobs and no friends that I can find. You even had to live with your brother all your adult life."

"I told you he was disabled," she said. The smile had now gone.

"He wasn't always, though, I see. In fact, he only lost the use of his legs after an accident. What a coincidence? It just happens to be the accident that killed Celia Hanson."

"Stephanie shrugged. "As I said, my brother was driving. It was nothing to do with me. And do you know, it could have been him that killed those poor nurses? Now I think of it, he had met Doreen and Lillian Yin."

"So that's what you're going with, is it?"

"Makes sense to me."

Johnson banged his fist on the table. "So how the hell did he manage to kill young Latham if he'd been dead for four hours?"

Stephanie Epsom smiled sweetly. "Well, he must have simply fallen then after all."

Mills asked a question. "Let's go back to Lillian Yin's death. You said you saw her next to her car after you left work."

"Yes, that's correct. I glanced over and saw her cry out and hold her chest, so I ran over to help her. I tried to save her for a good few minutes. The doctor turned up too late."

"But we have evidence that she died immediately, some minutes earlier, so why were you pretending to save her? Was it so you had a witness to the death?"

"There's no way you could know if she died before then, Sergeant. You weren't there." He couldn't explain that. Bennett had told him that an anonymous source had told him in confidence that it was true. He had a feeling it was his wife, but would rather not know.

"Let me ask you this then, what were you doing in the carpark?"

"What was I doing? I was looking for my brother."

"We've checked. You either walked home or he picked you up out the front. So I ask you again, what were you doing in the carpark? Because you don't drive yourself, do you? That's why you had to get your brother to drive when you followed Celia that day. How many times did you have to follow her before you found the right moment to do it?" asked Mills.

"That's for you to find out. Do you really think I am going to admit it? So you're saying I killed three nurses, a journalist, and my own brother just because I didn't get a job?"

"That's exactly what we are saying," answered Sergeant Mills.

"Then again, perhaps I should plead insanity. I could go to a hospital and let someone look after me for the rest of my life for a change."

DCI Johnson shouted back at her, "That will never happen. I'm going to make sure you rot in jail for what you've done." Making him look daft in front of everyone, he was thinking. Not only did he have to make a full report for the CC, he was going to have to do another press conference. This time explaining why he arrested the wrong man and how they missed the fact that there had been two nurses murdered and they hadn't even noticed. He'd get the evidence to get her banged up if he had to plant it in her house himself!

Chapter 25

ON FRIDAY MORNING, THE DEADLY DETECTIVE Agency had a special meeting at Hayley's house. They had heard that Stephanie Epsom had been arrested and charged, but they wanted all the gossip and news. Hayley had been to the newsagents and was going to do a special reading of The Chiltern Weekly article on the case. They were all there, even Luna, apart from young Suzie and Tiggy.

"If you're all sitting comfortably, then I'll begin." Luna sure was; she was curled up, fast asleep on Hayley's lap. "Celia, there's a lovely photo of you and an awful one of Epsom." She held the paper up so they could all see. "I'll read the headline first:

WOMAN ARRESTED FOR MURDER OF NURSE
& JOURNALIST

Sixty-year-old Stephanie Epsom of
Belford Avenue, Gorebridge, has
been charged with the murders of
Josh Latham and Celia Hanson.
Josh's body was discovered on May
11th at Gorebridge General
Hospital. A forensic post-mortem
examination determined he had
died of head injuries, said a
police statement from Detective
Chief Inspector Tony Johnson.

Celia Hanson was killed when a
car driven by Epsom's brother,
the late Lewis Epsom and also the
accused, deliberately collided
with her car on the M1 in 2020.

A forensic search of Epsom's home
found incriminating evidence.
Epsom had worked at Gorebridge
General Hospital for over 25
years, and colleagues were
shocked by the news of her
arrest.

Josh Latham, 34, was a trainee
nurse and formerly a fireman. The
Gorebridge Fire Service has
expressed their sadness at the
news. He had been forced to leave
after an injury.

Epsom has been remanded into
custody and will appear in court
on Wednesday. Other charges are
expected to follow.

The Chiltern Weekly would like to
express their devastation to
learn that their much-loved
reporter, Celia Hanson, had been
murdered. She was doing an
exclusive on deaths at Gorebridge
General Hospital at the time. The
deaths of two nurses, Doreen Gray
and Lillian Yin, are to be re-
opened thanks to Celia. A
memorial will take place shortly,
and this paper will give you more
details of her bravery and
tenacity in the near future.

OLIVER PICKETT, EDITOR.

So there you are. The beginning of the end for another murderer. Mostly thanks to you, Celia."

"Thanks to all of us, Hayley," said a very happy Celia.

Lillian put her hand to her mouth. "You don't know how nice it is to hear my name being used in the real world. I thought I would have been forgotten by now. It's not even about justice; it's about being remembered and that someone cares."

Terry took her hand. "I'm happy for you, love. Brilliant work, Abigail." And this time he meant it. He wished he could be remembered. He imagined it would be a perfect feeling. He wondered if Abigail could help him to find out about himself. They were getting on a lot better these days. He even thought they could be something more than friends but decided that would never happen; he hadn't exactly treated her well lately.

Terry always assumed he had no family at all. But he must have had parents. What if he had brothers and sisters? Somehow he always had an affinity with farmers. He had felt it when he had been to those old cottages where Janette lived. He had the feeling that once he hadn't doffed his hat when the Lady of the manor had been driven past in her carriage, and he had got the ruler across the palm of his hand the next day at school. That wasn't when he was living at the orphanage. Where had he been living then? It was a mystery, and there was no one better to get him the truth than Abigail and Hayley. He'd been dead for so long, he couldn't even remember if he had family before he had gone to the Barnardo's home for orphans. He might have had uncles and aunts or brothers or sisters. He stopped daydreaming as Betty had asked Hayley what incriminating evidence had been found at the house.

"Tom went with them to search, and in the drawer under her bed, they found syringes and a drug called Entrinatron which may have caused the deaths to look like heart attacks. Now they have got something to check for. She'd obviously pinched it from the pharmacy. There was no smoking dagger, as you say, Betty. But after the interview, Johnson insisted that they had to go back and check the house again, in case they had missed something, and you'll never guess what they found?"

"No, I won't; tell us quickly," pleaded Betty.

"In the back of a drawer, there was a piece of paper, and on it was Celia's name, address, and the make and model of her car. And not only that, her number plate as well."

"So they've got her for Celia's death and the motive for yours, Josh. Happy days," exclaimed Abigail. "Thank goodness Johnson sent them back to check the house again. Maybe there is hope for him."

Hayley had her suspicions about the timing of Johnson's brilliance and the finding of the crucial evidence. "Tom was surprised as well, I can tell you. He doesn't think they'll even look into the brother's murder, but they are talking about exhuming Doreen and looking at the others. But this is what is interesting; she's talking about pleading insanity."

"Well, she's not wrong, is she?" said Lillian. "As long as she admits to all the murders, that would be enough for me. What about you, Celia?"

"I would quite enjoy a court case, but I suppose it would get justice for everyone."

"Yes. Tom said she would have to admit to all four murders and maybe even her brother's. To be honest, it would be better for us at the agency, as there could be some awkward questions asked about how the other deaths were questioned and how Tom knew that she was lying over the time of death. Because that was what started it all off, and Celia talking to Josh, and he felt something go in his back just before he fell. Otherwise, his death would have just been a young nurse working too hard and rushing down the stairs. Tom can hardly say he had information from a dead detective and reporter through his psychic wife."

Celia had to agree. "Not forgetting a note typed on an editor's computer from the dead reporter. As long as she's locked up for good, I can live with that."

"Don't you start with the jokes as well," laughed Terry.

"I'm sure she will be," said Hayley. "But that's not the only good news in the paper today. There's a small bit on page five about the Not So Honourable Charles Hatton." That got them all on the edge of their seats. "He is due to appear in court on September 22nd at Gorebridge Crown Court."

"Fantastic news," said Abigail. "I have a feeling we will all have front row seats."

"I'm not sure if I want to go," said Lillian. "I still get hurt when I think of Jim. I really liked him. If it wasn't for Charles, he would never have killed anyone. I'm sorry, Abigail."

"You're absolutely right. He was basically a good person and just made a very bad decision. Funnily enough, I don't blame him so much as Charles. If it hadn't been Jim, he would have found someone else."

Betty thought so as well. "Jim was broke and lonely at the time. I think he saw it as a way to get away from life."

"Well, he got his wish," said Terry, smiling. "I don't think I'd be as forgiving as you, Abigail. But saying that, he got a punishment far worse than Charles will get. For now anyway. That reminds me, Hayley, did you hear any more from Janette about her haunting?"

"No. I can't tell her you checked her house and didn't see anyone, but I'll tell her I'll visit and see for myself. I'll do it now." Abigail began tapping on her phone to send the email. "Dear Janette. I have some free time and will come round this evening to see if I can help you with your problem, send... That's quick, she's answered already...Dear Hayley. No point coming tonight, I only see them in the daytime while I am at work. I could meet you there tomorrow after work at about six o'clock."

"That's weird," said Terry.

"Where is that?" typed Hayley.

"The Becklesfield Public Library," Janette - the librarian - typed back.

"Oh my giddy aunt," said Betty. They all started laughing and talking at the same time.

"That's hilarious. It was us scaring that poor woman to death. I didn't have a clue she thought it was haunted," said Abigail. "We're going to have to be more careful and use the reference room more. And we'll need to make more flyers and posters saying the Detective Agency is only open after midnight. Seriously, what are the chances of that? Of all the mediums in the world, she clicks on to yours. That in itself is kinda spooky. And when you think about it, we have solved another case for someone, albeit by chance. I've lost count now, but as you know, I'm not one to blow my own trumpet."

Terry really started laughing at that. "Ha. You blow your own trumpet more than Kenny Ball."

"I've no idea who that is, Terry, but assume he didn't play much," snapped Abigail.

Betty jumped in quickly. "Oh no, dear, he was a brilliant musician. I loved Kenny Ball and his Jazzmen."

"Well thank you very much, Betty. I thought you were my friend," said Abigail and started laughing too. What with all the murders and investigations, laughter and fun had somehow been forgotten. It was a lovely moment for all of them.

Hayley put her hand over her mouth and gasped. "Oh my God, folks. I've just thought of something I'd forgotten. Janette told me in her first email that it wasn't just ghosts, there was a strange, crazy woman that she couldn't get away from. That was me! That day in the library she more or less said that I was as mad as a March hare for talking to myself, do you remember? I blame you lot. You'll get me carted off in the end."

"It's funny but I can't help feeling a bit sorry for her," said Betty. "I think we should keep away from the library when she's there. I would like to apologise, but that would frighten her. Perhaps you can tell her, Hayley dear."

"I obviously can't meet her tomorrow. I'm surprised she didn't recognize me on the website. But I did put a nice photo on there from my younger days. I should be a bit hurt that she didn't think it was me. I'll have to say I've had a message that the ghosts have gone and won't be bothering her again, and actually that's true when you think about it. Shows how careful we have to be."

Abigail and the others said they would try to be a bit more thoughtful in the future so she didn't look quite so weird. But Hayley had to admit that ship had sailed long before they had come into her life!

"I have got some more good news that I'm so excited to share with you," said Hayley. "This was totally out of the blue. I had a phone call from Lady Caroline Hatton inviting me to tea on Monday."

"What on earth is that about, I wonder?" said Abigail.

"She had heard a rumour from people that I had helped with

the case against Charles, would you believe? And now she is settled in Chiltern Hall, she wants to meet some other people in the area and thank me. Helen and Angus have moved to Scotland and she's inheriting everything now. They're not living in the main house, but she's letting them stay in the small lodge up there, which is really good of her. She didn't have to, but it shows the kind of person she is. She wants to have a reading as well while I'm there. Could be she wants to try and contact her parents. She was very young when they died. I've no idea how she knew about me, or us, I should say."

"I bet it's the Women's Institute."

"Or Oliver, my editor."

"Tom said the CC knows about the rumour that there's a psychic helping the police and he's all for it, as long as it's on the quiet. Apparently his wife is into that kind of thing."

"That's very handy," said Abigail. "We might need her on our side in the future."

"I wondered if you would come with me, Abigail? Just her, I'm afraid," she said to the others. "You don't know how hard it is to have a normal conversation when you are all there." The other detectives could all understand that and said they didn't mind at all.

"I'd love to come, Hayley. And I promise I will be as quiet as a church mouse." That really got them laughing!

Chapter 26

IT WAS A LOVELY DAY WHEN HAYLEY DROVE THE SHORT distance to Chiltern Hall. Arthur, the gardener, gave her a wave as she turned through the ornamental wrought-iron gates and started down the long driveway. He didn't know that she wasn't alone. Abigail sat excitedly next to her. "I wonder if you'll have cucumber sandwiches and Victoria Sponge. I wish I could have a slice of cake and a cup of tea. I don't feel hungry, but I still fancy one."

"Sounds like when I gave up smoking when I was a teenager. I wasn't even craving one, but I really wanted one. You have to think of other things. Like what on earth am I going to say to Caroline?"

"Could you tell her the truth? Perhaps not all of it. But that I had visited you and said I was murdered and take it from there."

"I'll play it by ear. It all depends on what vibes I get from her. If she's a sceptic, then forget it. I'll say it wasn't anything to do with me, and it was all down to Johnson's marvellous police work."

"You should at least say something believable," laughed Abigail.

"That's true. She brought it up, so I reckon she will be fine about it."

Hayley parked her little red Mini and walked up the stairs to the front door. She had never been inside and was looking forward to seeing the antique furniture and artwork. Before she could knock the door was opened.

"Come in, Madam," said Mrs Bittens, the housekeeper.

"Madams!" said Abigail.

"Lady Caroline is in the drawing room." She stood up to greet Hayley and took her hand. The new heir had beautiful auburn hair that was pulled to one side and cascaded over her shoulder in curls. Abigail could tell from the cut of her cream blouse and beige trousers that they were of a certain designer label. With her tall frame and perfect figure, she wouldn't have needed Abigail's skills to make them fit. Her blue eyes were framed with thick lashes, and although she had everything she wanted now, Abigail reckoned that she would have had the looks to be a film star.

"It's so lovely to meet you. I've heard nothing but good things about you. Your ears must have been burning the other night. I had a dinner party, and your name came up more than once. George Carson, the Chief Constable, was there. He tells me that your husband works for him, and his wife is a great fan. She had seen you at work when you told a young lady she was going to have a baby. Do sit down."

"Thank you, Lady Caroline."

"Just Caroline, please."

"That was at a WI talk that I gave. Her father came to me with a message for her."

"I find it all so fascinating. Although when I'm here on my own at night, I'm scared to death. It's the kind of house where it can be easy to think there are knights in armour walking about, or the odd monk walking through walls. I've heard of psychics that help the police, mainly on the TV, but I have to know, did you have anything to do with my cousin being caught? I can't tell you how grateful I am if you did. I'd still be penniless in London."

"Do you think you will give up acting now?"

"I'm not altogether sure, Hayley. It was hard work, but I miss the people, and I've been warned that running the estate can take a lot of time. But never say never."

"You've certainly got the looks for it. But if the May Day Fayre was anything to go by, then you've got your work cut out. Then there's the harvest festival and the other charity obligations. Have you heard any more about the court case?"

"I've been in contact with my solicitor, and she's been told that Charles still intends to plead not guilty, despite all the evidence against him. That's the trouble, money has always solved every problem he has ever had. I remember when he was at prep school, he nearly killed another boy when he put rat poison in his supper for a joke. He was going to be expelled until Uncle Angus paid for a new cricket pavilion and all was quietly swept under the carpet. Then there was the maid that had to be paid off when he was about seventeen. I'm still not sure what he did to her, but I can guess. He was always a spoiled brat and never knew the meaning of the word no. He still hasn't grown up at all, and it hasn't sunk in that he can't be protected by his mummy and daddy anymore. He's in for a shock according to my solicitor who thinks he is looking at a life sentence."

"I'll believe it when I see it. Money still talks, and Angus was a magistrate so he still might know the right people."

"I have a feeling Uncle might be looking at his own prison cell for fraud. I still find it hard to think they would diddle me out of my inheritance. It wasn't just the money, it was the lands and title. I would never have known if he hadn't killed that poor woman, Miss Summers, I think it was. I can remember Helen telling me over the phone, before anyone knew it was murder, that she was really upset that she had died and would miss her terribly - apparently good dressmakers are hard to find."

"Charming," said Abigail.

Hayley hesitated and looked at Abigail who was sitting on the sofa next to Caroline, opposite the wing-backed chair that she was sitting on. "Tell her. Go on," urged Abigail to Hayley.

She blew out her cheeks. "Well, I would rather this didn't go any further, but Abigail Summers came to me and told me she had been murdered and would I help her to work out who had killed her, so we did have a hand in it."

Caroline was excited and not at all surprised. "How fascinating. And she told you that it was this builder, Jim Tate or did she say Charles straightaway?"

"Well, not in so many words. She didn't know who did it, and to start with she had no clue that she had been murdered. Not until she found out that her CO2 alarms were missing. That was when she came to me. So we had to discount the people that Abigail had seen before she died. There were a few others as well, like her relatives. There was a dodgy accountant - by the way, don't have anything to do with Nathan Hill - but it wasn't him. Abigail was very busy with her sewing, and she actually came to the Hall a few days before she died and did a fitting for Helen, Angus, and Charles. She did it in the master bedroom. Abigail thought that she saw something that she had to die for."

"In my bedroom. Oh my. What was it?"

"There were a couple of photographs, and one was of your dad, which showed he was older than Angus. But she never even noticed it, really. Charles assumed that she had. And she told me she remembered there was a lovely landscape of a lake over the bed."

"The photo has gone. I don't ever remember seeing it. But the painting is of a loch on the estate in Scotland. I had it moved into here." They walked over to see its new place on the wall by the window.

"It's beautiful. No wonder Abigail loved it," said Hayley.

"It has a special meaning for me. See that boat there - it belongs to the estate. My parents loved going out for a sail on it."

"That's not the boat they lost their lives on, is it? Helen told me about it and said she was frightened of the water, that must be why."

"That's the one - the Asphodel - named after the flower. It was a cold day but no windier than it usually was, and they were both excellent sailors. They thought somehow my father was killed by the boom hitting his head, but he was always careful about that. And my mother's body was never found. They presume she went overboard when the boat tilted. She was a strong swimmer, so I've always had my doubts.

I was five and can just about remember Mummy and Daddy. This is them." They walked over to the piano, on which was a framed photograph of her red-haired father holding a baby and a very attractive woman, smiling. They were sitting on a sofa, and Caroline was dressed in a christening robe.

"She's beautiful," said Hayley. "I'm so sorry."

"It was just after my grandfather had died, as well. It's all come out now. They always told me my parents died first and daddy was the youngest. My whole life changed in one week. Tell me and be honest, do you think there's any way that the boat accident was something else, Hayley?"

"Let's ask the expert, shall we?" she answered.

"Tom?"

Hayley laughed. "Much as I would love to say yes, I mean someone else, who is standing next to you. Yep, that's right - Abigail!"

Caroline's eyes widened, but she wasn't at all frightened. "She really is here? How exciting. Can she hear me?"

"Of course. She says hi. So what do you think, Abi? Do you think her uncle and aunt could have had something to do with it?… She says definitely… But that doesn't mean they did. She had assumed it was just the hereditary dates they were hiding, but who knows. It was definitely good timing… She said, was the boat examined at the time?"

"Yes, it was. There was blood on the boom which was my father's, but nothing to say what happened to my mother. No blood on the rail or anything. The inquest ruled it as an accident. The wind could suddenly get up out there on the loch, and the sails could have tipped it over. They made a point of saying that neither of them was wearing a lifejacket. When they didn't come back, a search party was sent out in the dark, and they towed the boat back. They looked again the next day, but there was no sign of Mummy's body." She brushed a tear away.

"Abigail thinks too much time has passed and as far as she knows they wouldn't open the case. Any proof would be gone by now. And she says if she was you, she'd keep her distance from them. But you won't know for sure, one way or another. The fact that Helen talked about the boat could mean that she didn't have anything to do with it. I got a feeling of fright but not worry or guilt."

"Mummy would never have left me and Daddy, so I know she's dead. That was something else I wanted to ask you, Hayley, do you think you could get through to her? I know it's asking a lot. You see, I was able to say goodbye to my father at the funeral, but I never had closure with Mummy."

"I totally understand. I probably won't be able to do that now. I don't sense she's here, but I will definitely keep trying. What was her name, just in case she comes to me when she's ready?"

"Georgina."

. . .

Abigail and Hayley both looked at each other. They remembered May Day and thought back to when Terry had gone to look for the missing toddler, Dexter, by the river.

"That was her name, wasn't it? She was by the river, waiting for someone. She was looking after the little boys, Lenny and something," said Abigail excitedly.

"It was, hun. You couldn't write about it, could you?"

"What?" asked a confused Caroline.

"I'm sorry. Abigail and I have heard the name Georgina, very recently. Did you hear that at the May Day Fayre a little boy went missing?"

"I did. And your husband found him."

"That's right. When Terry, another, you know, went to the river to look for him, he met a lady and two little boys, brothers, I believe. They had all passed. Terry asked if they wanted me to help them move on, but the boys were waiting for their mum and dad and the lady, who was called Georgina was waiting for someone as well - a young girl, I believe. Now that may be a coincidence, but I feel it in my bones that she is waiting for you."

Hayley was not expecting for Caroline to burst into floods of tears. She looked awkwardly at Abigail, and they wondered what to do. She saw some tissues on the sideboard and got one for her.

"Here you are, hun. I'm so sorry, it must be an awful shock for you."

"It's...the...best...thing that's ever happened to me. Can you believe my mum is waiting for me? And I haven't even offered you your tea..." she said in between sobs.

"Oh, please don't worry about that. Would you like us to go and see if she's still there? I can't promise anything. We might have to get Terry to tell us where she is. But I have a feeling she will always be waiting by water."

"Would you mind if I went and freshened up a bit? I feel a

right mess, and no doubt I'm all red from blubbering. Excuse me, please."

"We'd better be right," said Abigail after Caroline had left the room. "It might be Georgina Bloggs for all we know."

"Don't even say it, hun. Can you imagine?"

"Yes, I can. You'll have to say we've just missed her and make something up."

"I can't do that. Hopefully, it is her. What did Terry say about her?"

Abigail said, "If only he had come. I'm sure he said she was wearing modern clothes but the boys were from way back. Doesn't look like you'll be getting a cucumber sandwich either. She's very nice, isn't she?"

"She's lovely... She's coming," Hayley whispered.

Caroline had put on a pink chiffon dress and some lipstick and flat sandals in place of the cream high-heeled shoes. Now Hayley really felt the pressure.

"She might not be there, Caroline. Don't get your hopes up too much, please."

"I know, Hayley. It won't be your fault if she isn't. I promise I'll get Mrs Bittens to bring in tea as soon as we get back. I must be the world's worst host." They left the drawing room through the French windows and took the steps down to the lawn and followed the path to the river.

Abigail frowned and said, "Didn't Terry mention a summerhouse or something?"

"Is there a summerhouse by the river, Caroline?"

"Not that I know of... there's the old boathouse, of course. It's been there as long as the house, I'll show you."

Abigail walked on ahead and then turned around with a big smile on her face. "I can see them. Tell her she looks just like her mum."

"Oh Caroline, they are there. I wish you could see them. Abigail says you look just like your mum."

"I'm going to start crying again if you're not careful. Where is she?" They saw the boathouse first. It was an old wooden building badly in need of repair. Inside was an old rowing boat in a similar state and in which the two boys were playing.

Georgina turned around and only had to say two words for Hayley to know she had been right. "My baby."

It was Abigail's and Hayley's turn to cry then. "It's her, Caroline. She said 'my baby'."

"Mummy, I've missed you so much. Can she hear me?"

"She can. She says she can't believe how beautiful you are and how happy she is to see you again. She's asking if you are happy?"

Georgina went over to her daughter and touched her cheek. Caroline jumped for a second and then smiled. "I can feel her. Mummy, it really is you. I've missed you so much. And I am so happy now that we've met again. For the first time, I can get on with life. There was always a part of me that expected you to walk in the door. Or when I was out, I was looking for you constantly, and sometimes I'd even ask a lady what her name was if she looked like you. Are you alright, Mummy?"

"She is now she's seen you again and feels the same. Now that she knows you are all grown up and happy, she wants to move on and be with Graham."

"I can understand that. They were madly in love; everyone said. Could we sit and talk a while longer, though?"

"She's laughing and said she has waited years, so a bit longer won't hurt."

Abigail said she would take the two brothers, Lenny and Albert, for a walk to give them some privacy. Hopefully, Georgina would take them with her when she was ready to go. Hayley would need to explain that Mum and Dad were not coming and that they were waiting for them on the other side of the river. She held them both by the hand and walked across the landscaped lawns towards the house to look at the lovely flowers that were in bloom. The boys weren't at all interested in them, so ran towards a large cedar tree that was perfect for climbing.

She was just thinking what a lovely day it was to be dead when she saw someone walking through the violet hydrangeas and coming towards her.

"I say, Miss, do you think you could help me?" He was a blond-haired man who was smartly dressed for tennis. Going by the cream trousers, Abigail dated his clothes to the 1930s. In one hand, he held his wooden racquet, and the other was holding a pair of pruning shears, that unfortunately for him were protruding from his torso. The bright red blood covered the front of his cable-knit jumper.

"Uh-oh," said Abigail. "Here we go again."

THE END

About the Author

Ann Parker was born in Hertfordshire, England and still lives there, in a haunted cottage with her husband, Terry, and her black and white cat, Jazz.

She is the author of the Abigail Summers Cosy Mysteries and the short story book entitled Magic & Memories. Ann has had poems published on Spillwords and in the best selling anthology Hidden in Childhood as well as various magazines.

When she is not writing, she loves to spend time with her family or reading a good whodunnit.

———————

To learn more about Ann Parker and discover more Next Chapter authors, visit our website at www.nextchapter.pub.

Printed in Great Britain
by Amazon

33002633R00118